D0990329

STONE ARCH BOOKS
a capstone imprint

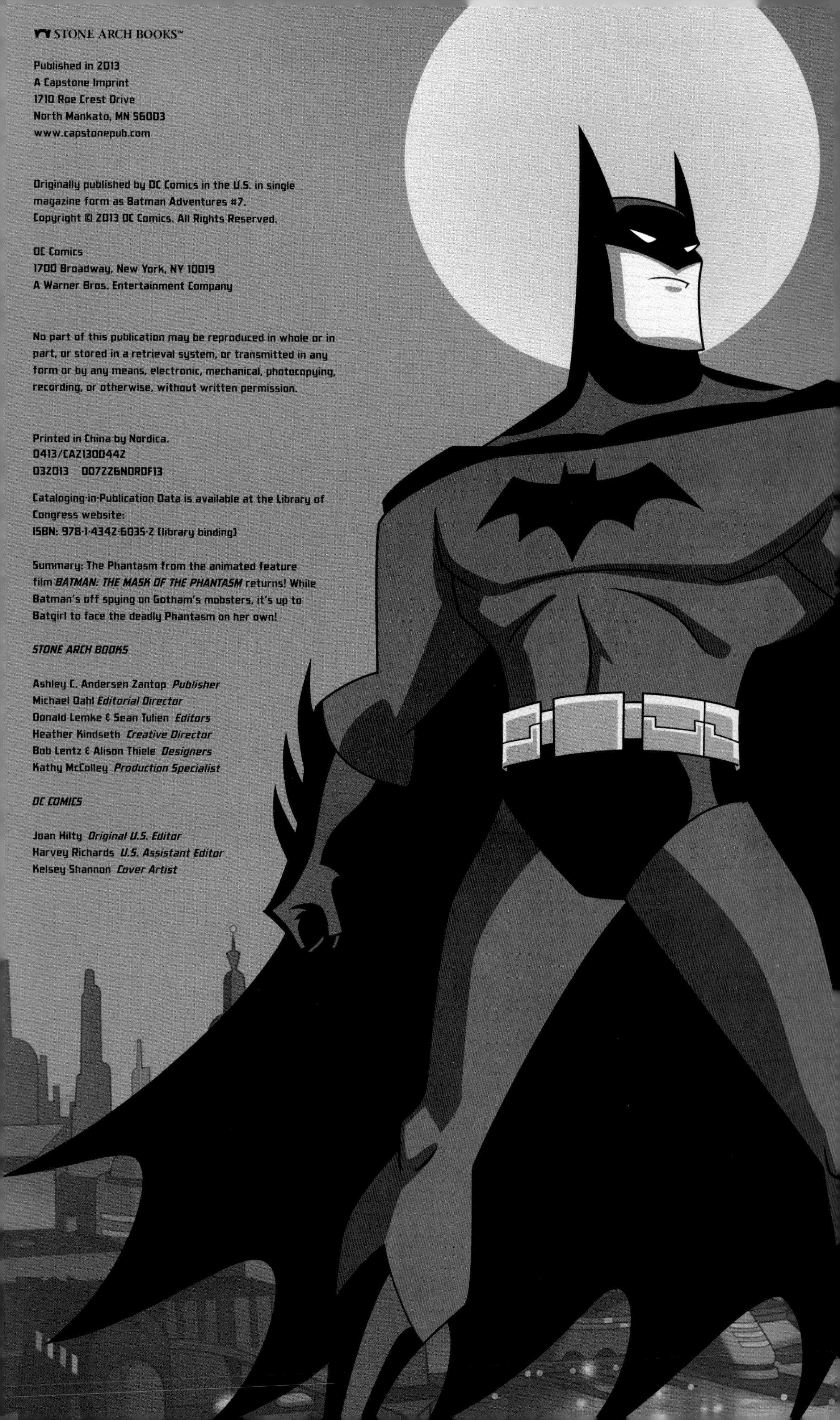

STONE ARCH BOOKS™

Published in 2013
A Capstone Imprint
1710 Roe Crest Drive
North Mankato, MN 56003
www.capstonepub.com

Originally published by DC Comics in the U.S. in single magazine form as Batman Adventures #7.

DC Comics
1700 Broadway, New York, NY 10019
A Warner Bros. Entertainment Company

Printed in China by Nordica.
0413/CA21300442
032013 007226NORDF13

Cataloging-in-Publication Data is available at the Library of Congress website:
ISBN: 978-1-4342-6035-2 (library binding)

Summary: The Phantasm from the animated feature film ***BATMAN: THE MASK OF THE PHANTASM*** returns! While Batman's off spying on Gotham's mobsters, it's up to Batgirl to face the deadly Phantasm on her own!

STONE ARCH BOOKS

Ashley C. Andersen Zantop *Publisher*
Michael Dahl *Editorial Director*
Donald Lemke & Sean Tulien *Editors*
Heather Kindseth *Creative Director*
Bob Lentz & Alison Thiele *Designers*
Kathy McColley *Production Specialist*

DC COMICS

Joan Hilty *Original U.S. Editor*
Harvey Richards *U.S. Assistant Editor*
Kelsey Shannon *Cover Artist*

BATMAN ADVENTURES

PHANTASM STRIKES!

Dan Slott...writer
Rick Burchett ....penciller
Terry Beatty...inker
Lee Loughridge..colorist
Nick Napolitano.......................................letterer

**Batman created by
Bob Kane**

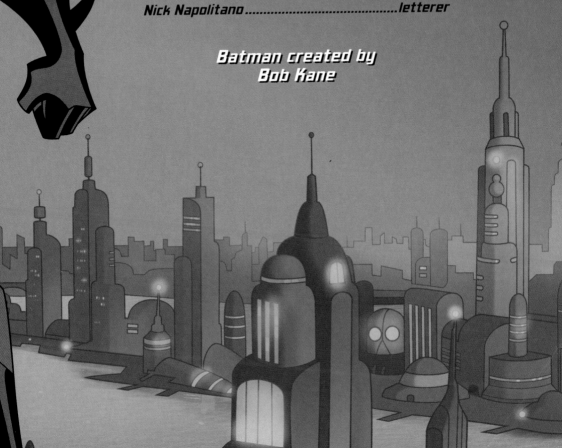

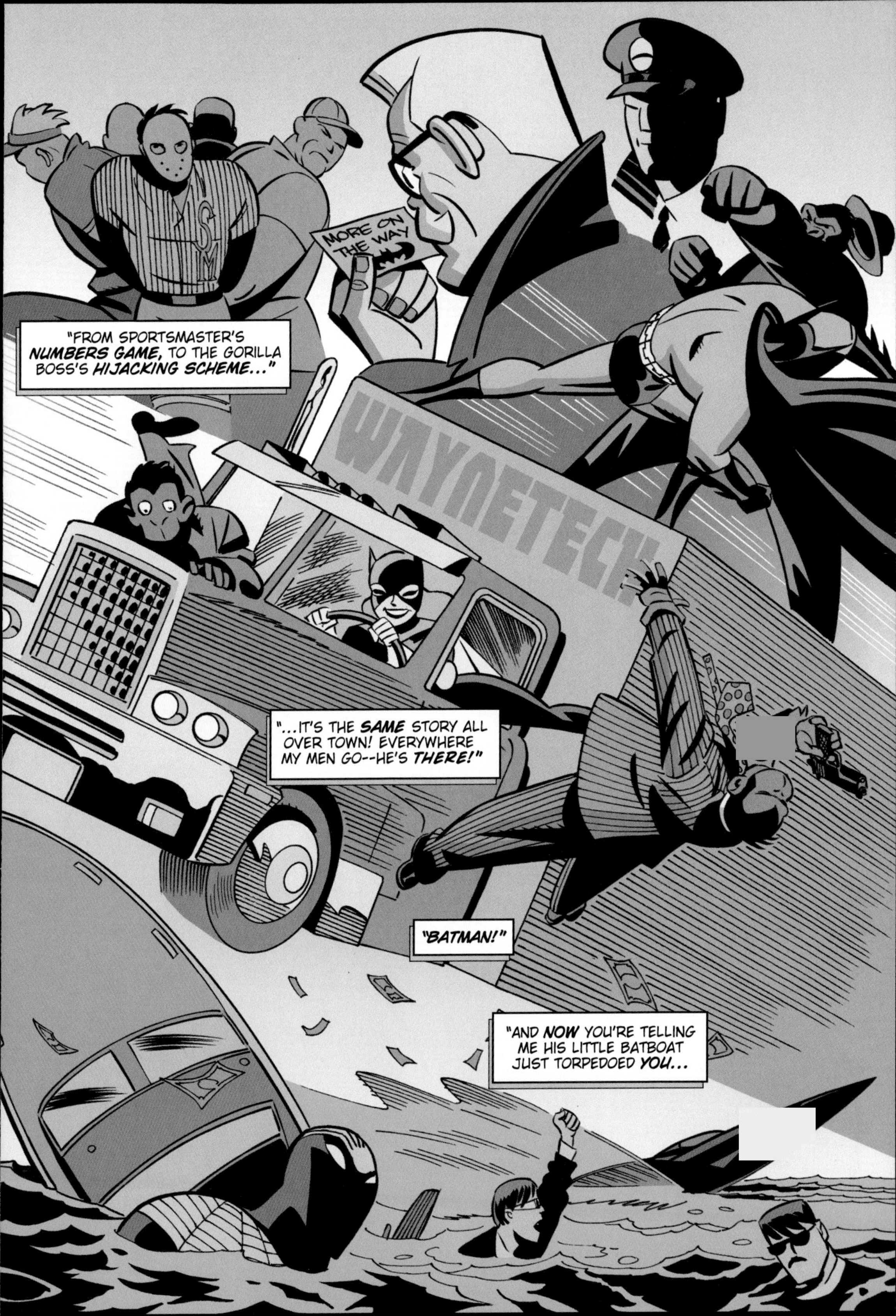
MORE ON THE WAY
"FROM SPORTSMASTER'S NUMBERS GAME, TO THE GORILLA BOSS'S HIJACKING SCHEME..."
WAYNETECH
"...IT'S THE SAME STORY ALL OVER TOWN! EVERYWHERE MY MEN GO--HE'S THERE!"
"BATMAN!"
"AND NOW YOU'RE TELLING ME HIS LITTLE BATBOAT JUST TORPEDOED YOU...

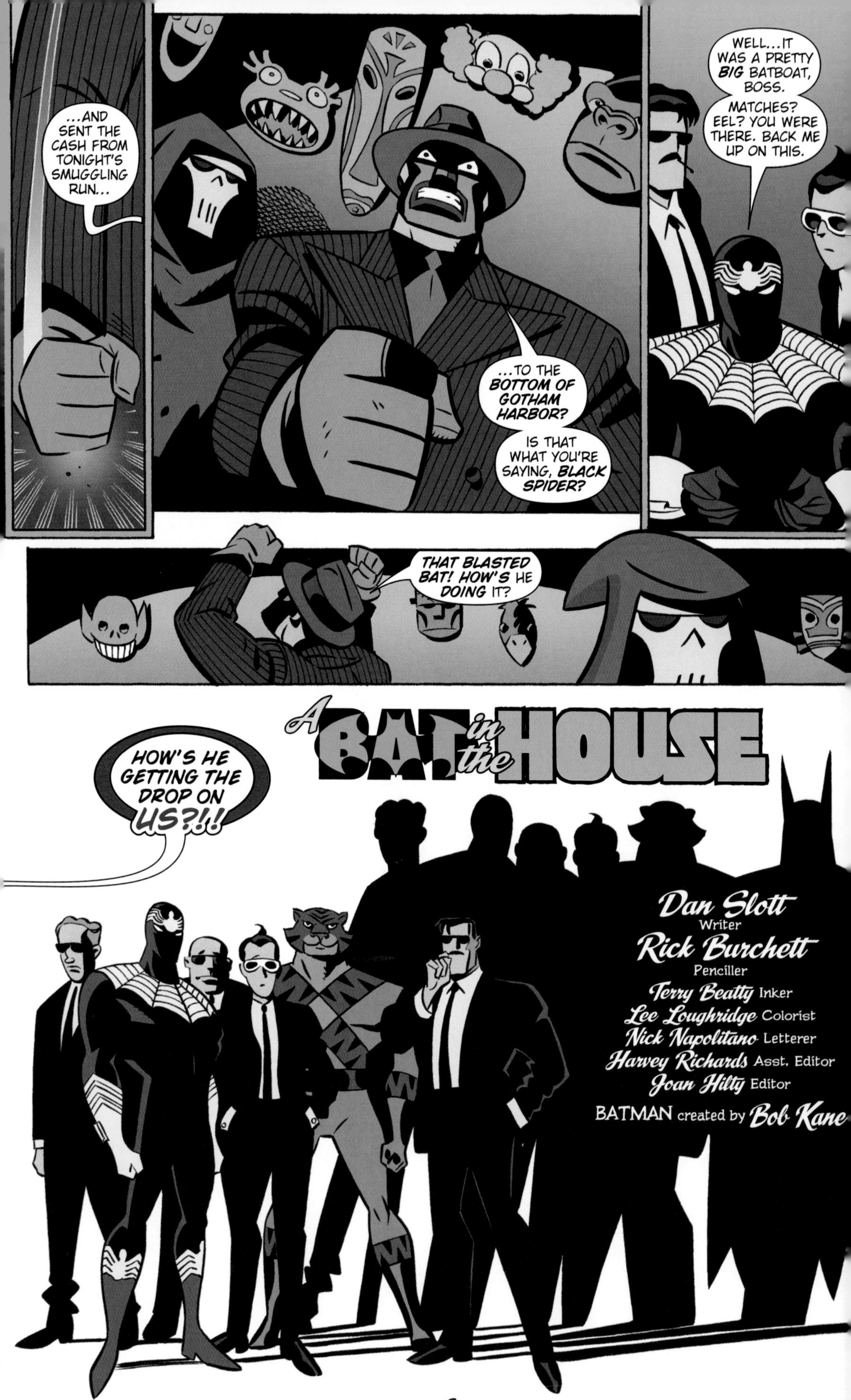
...AND SENT THE CASH FROM TONIGHT'S SMUGGLING RUN...
...TO THE BOTTOM OF GOTHAM HARBOR?
IS THAT WHAT YOU'RE SAYING, BLACK SPIDER?
WELL...IT WAS A PRETTY BIG BATBOAT, BOSS.
MATCHES? EEL? YOU WERE THERE. BACK ME UP ON THIS.
THAT BLASTED BAT! HOW'S HE DOING IT?
HOW'S HE GETTING THE DROP ON US?!!
A BAT in the HOUSE
Dan Slott Writer
Rick Burchett Penciller
Terry Beatty Inker
Lee Loughridge Colorist
Nick Napolitano Letterer
Harvey Richards Asst. Editor
Joan Hilty Editor
BATMAN created by Bob Kane

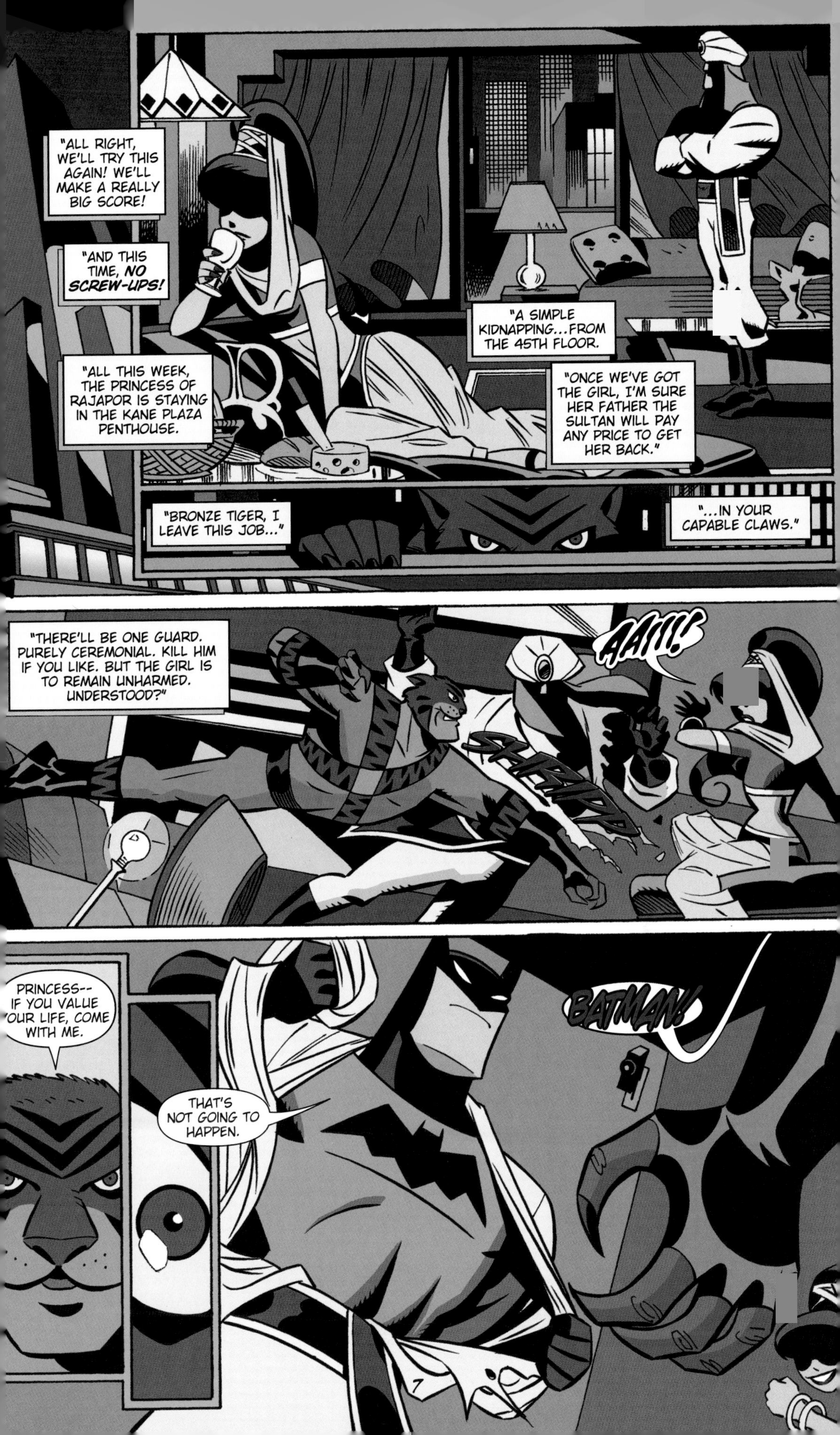
"ALL RIGHT, WE'LL TRY THIS AGAIN! WE'LL MAKE A REALLY BIG SCORE!
"AND THIS TIME, NO SCREW-UPS!
"ALL THIS WEEK, THE PRINCESS OF RAJAPOR IS STAYING IN THE KANE PLAZA PENTHOUSE.
"A SIMPLE KIDNAPPING...FROM THE 45TH FLOOR.
"ONCE WE'VE GOT THE GIRL, I'M SURE HER FATHER THE SULTAN WILL PAY ANY PRICE TO GET HER BACK."
"BRONZE TIGER, I LEAVE THIS JOB..."
"...IN YOUR CAPABLE CLAWS."
"THERE'LL BE ONE GUARD. PURELY CEREMONIAL. KILL HIM IF YOU LIKE. BUT THE GIRL IS TO REMAIN UNHARMED. UNDERSTOOD?"
AAIII!
SHRRIPP
PRINCESS-- IF YOU VALUE OUR LIFE, COME WITH ME.
BATMAN!
THAT'S NOT GOING TO HAPPEN.

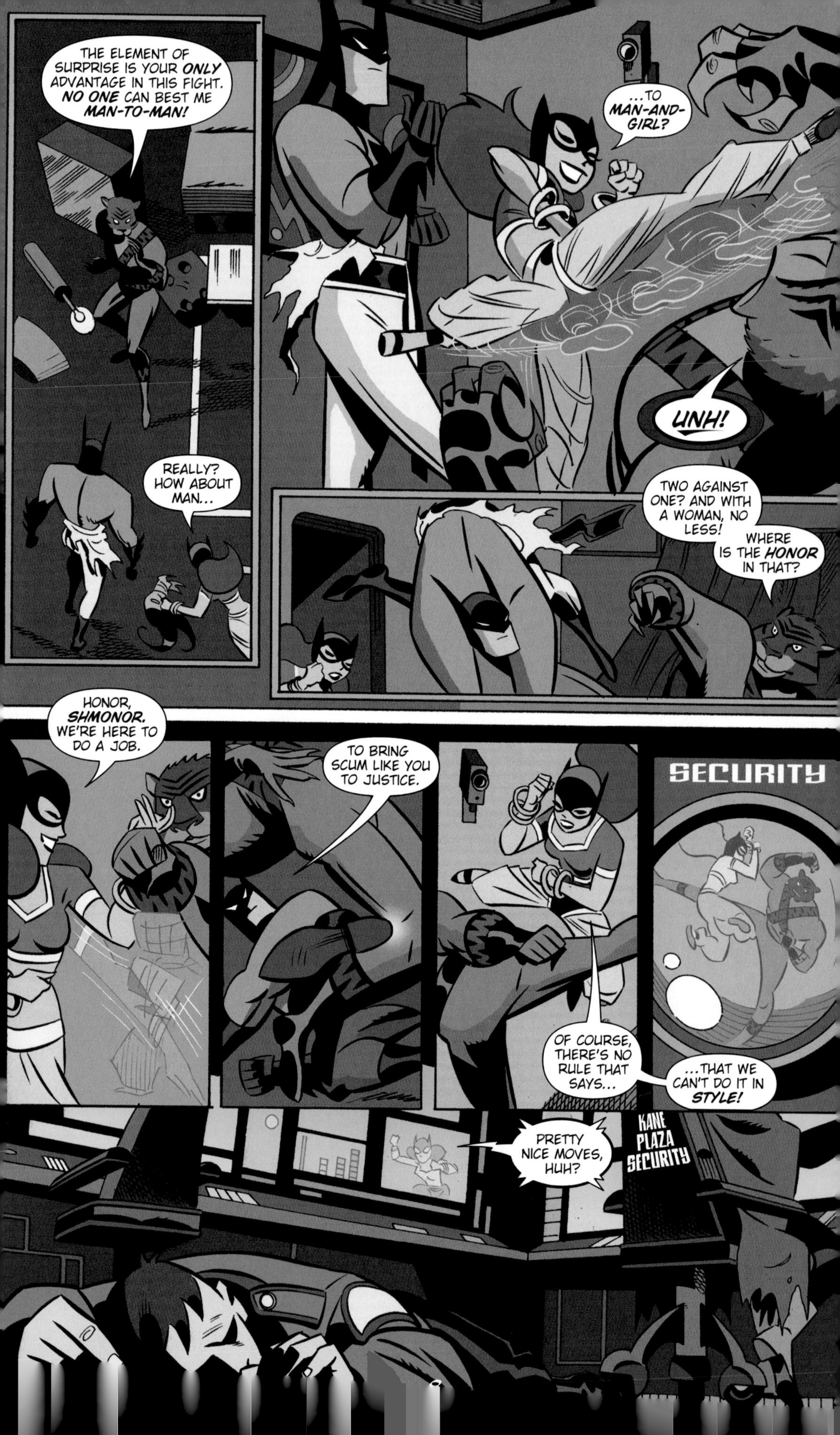
THE ELEMENT OF SURPRISE IS YOUR ONLY ADVANTAGE IN THIS FIGHT. NO ONE CAN BEST ME MAN-TO-MAN!
REALLY? HOW ABOUT MAN...
...TO MAN-AND-GIRL?
UNH!
TWO AGAINST ONE? AND WITH A WOMAN, NO LESS!
WHERE IS THE HONOR IN THAT?
HONOR, SHMONOR. WE'RE HERE TO DO A JOB.
TO BRING SCUM LIKE YOU TO JUSTICE.
SECURITY
OF COURSE, THERE'S NO RULE THAT SAYS...
...THAT WE CAN'T DO IT IN STYLE!
PRETTY NICE MOVES, HUH?
KANE PLAZA SECURITY

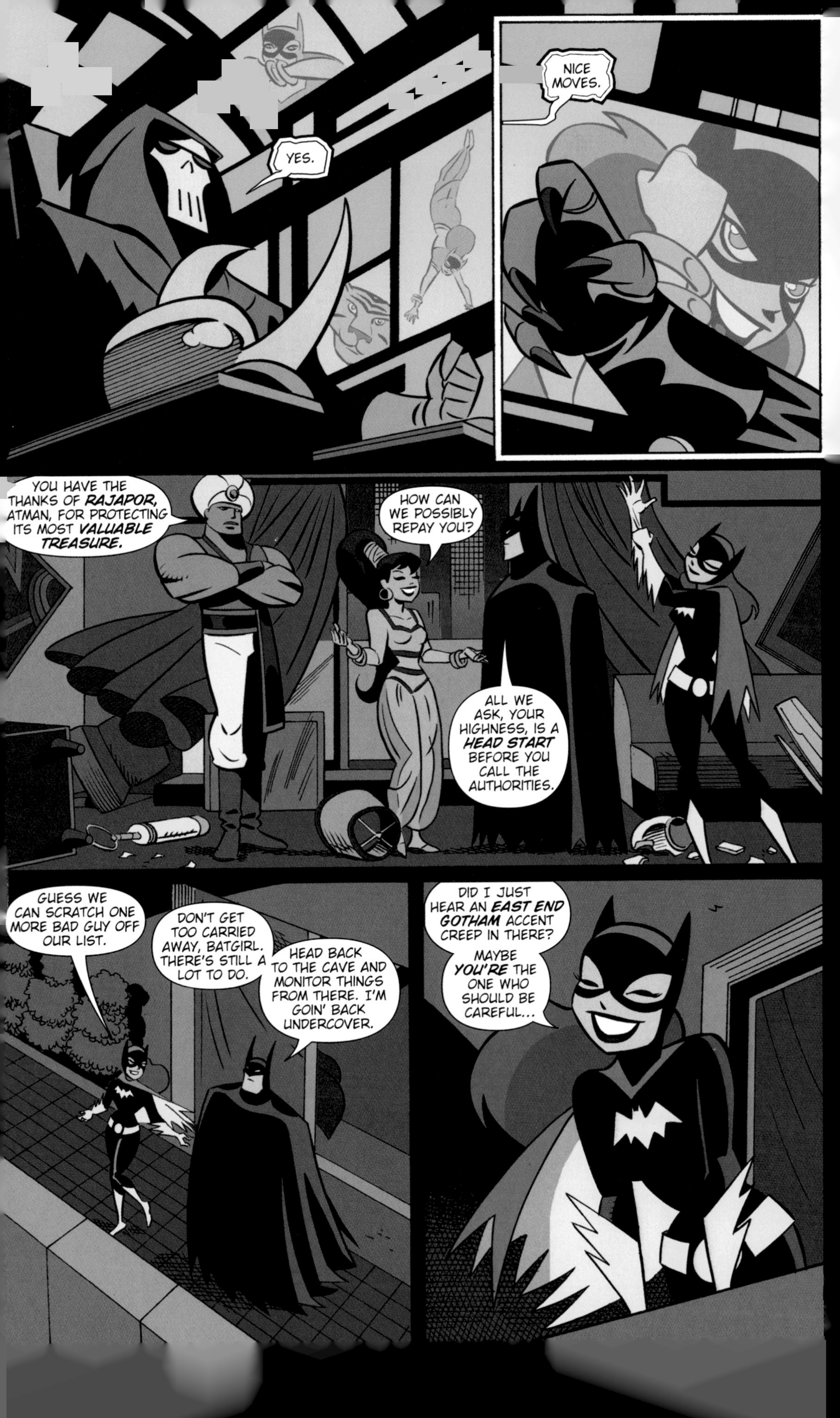
YES.
NICE MOVES.
YOU HAVE THE THANKS OF RAJAPOR, ATMAN, FOR PROTECTING ITS MOST VALUABLE TREASURE.
HOW CAN WE POSSIBLY REPAY YOU?
ALL WE ASK, YOUR HIGHNESS, IS A HEAD START BEFORE YOU CALL THE AUTHORITIES.
GUESS WE CAN SCRATCH ONE MORE BAD GUY OFF OUR LIST.
DON'T GET TOO CARRIED AWAY, BATGIRL. THERE'S STILL A LOT TO DO.
HEAD BACK TO THE CAVE AND MONITOR THINGS FROM THERE. I'M GOIN' BACK UNDERCOVER.
DID I JUST HEAR AN EAST END GOTHAM ACCENT CREEP IN THERE?
MAYBE YOU'RE THE ONE WHO SHOULD BE CAREFUL...

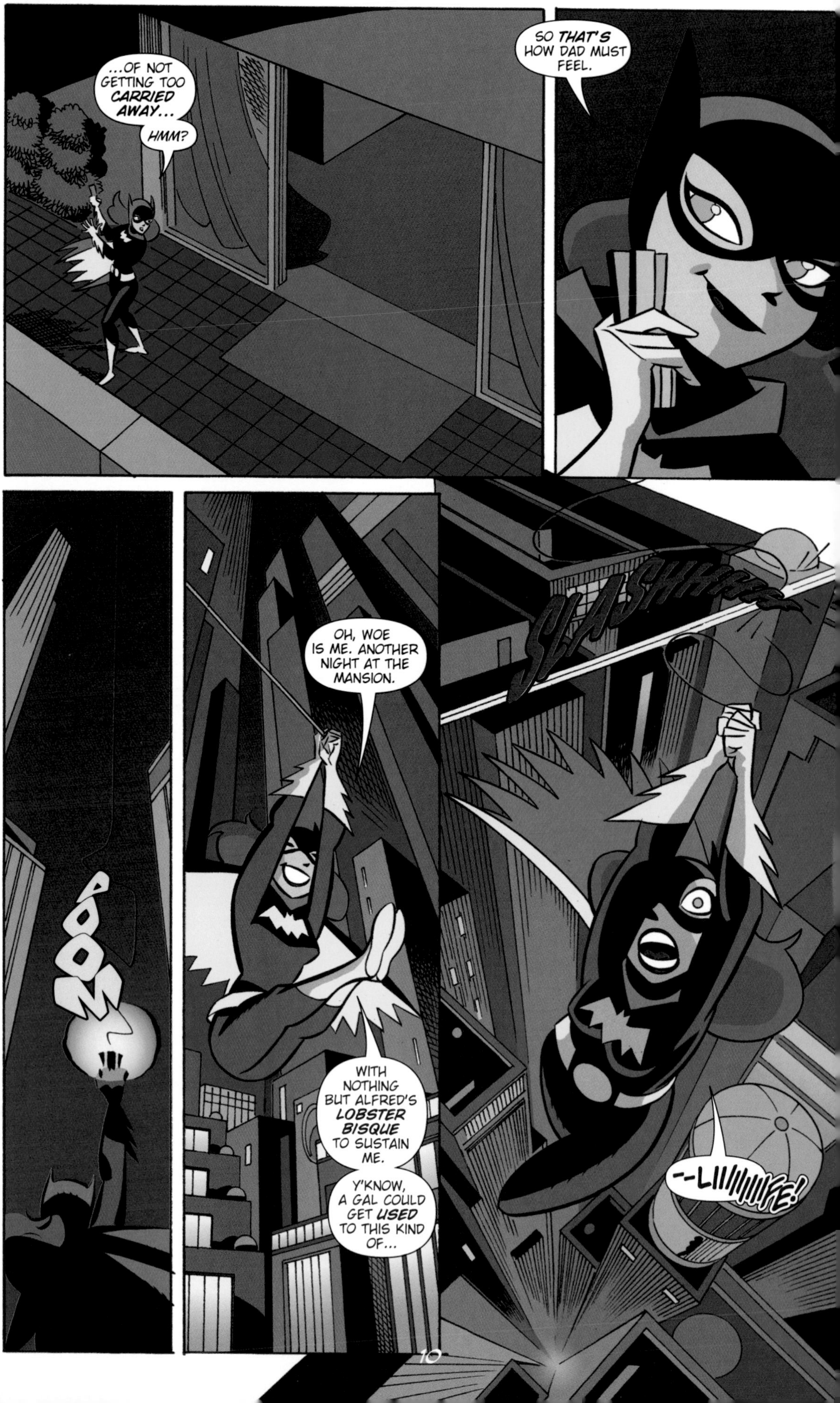
...OF NOT GETTING TOO CARRIED AWAY...
HMM?
SO THAT'S HOW DAD MUST FEEL.
POOM
OH, WOE IS ME. ANOTHER NIGHT AT THE MANSION.
WITH NOTHING BUT ALFRED'S LOBSTER BISQUE TO SUSTAIN ME.
Y'KNOW, A GAL COULD GET USED TO THIS KIND OF...
SLASHHHH
--LIIIIIIIIFE!

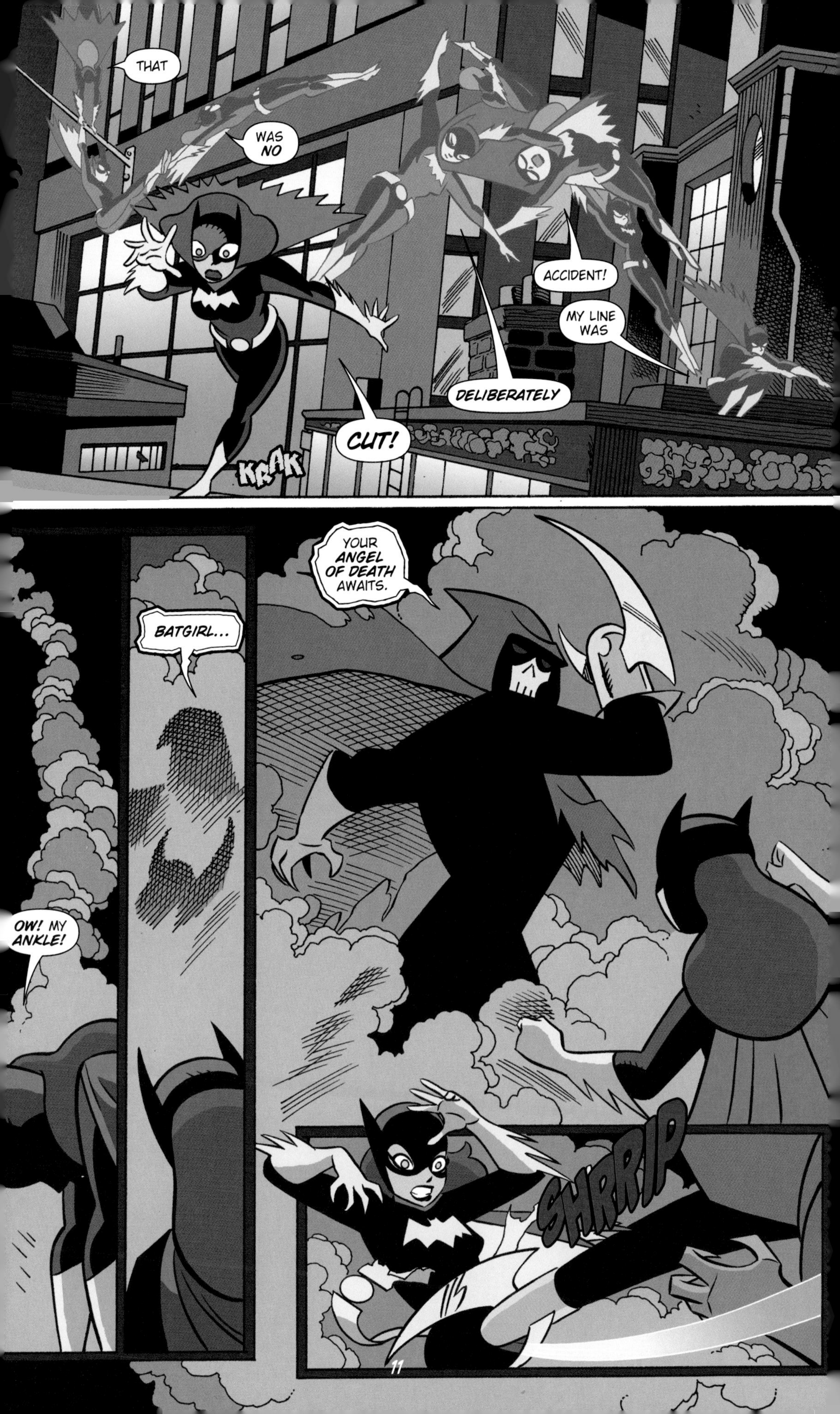

THAT
WAS NO
ACCIDENT!
MY LINE WAS
DELIBERATELY
CUT!
KRAK
YOUR ANGEL OF DEATH AWAITS.
BATGIRL...
OW! MY ANKLE!
SHRRIP

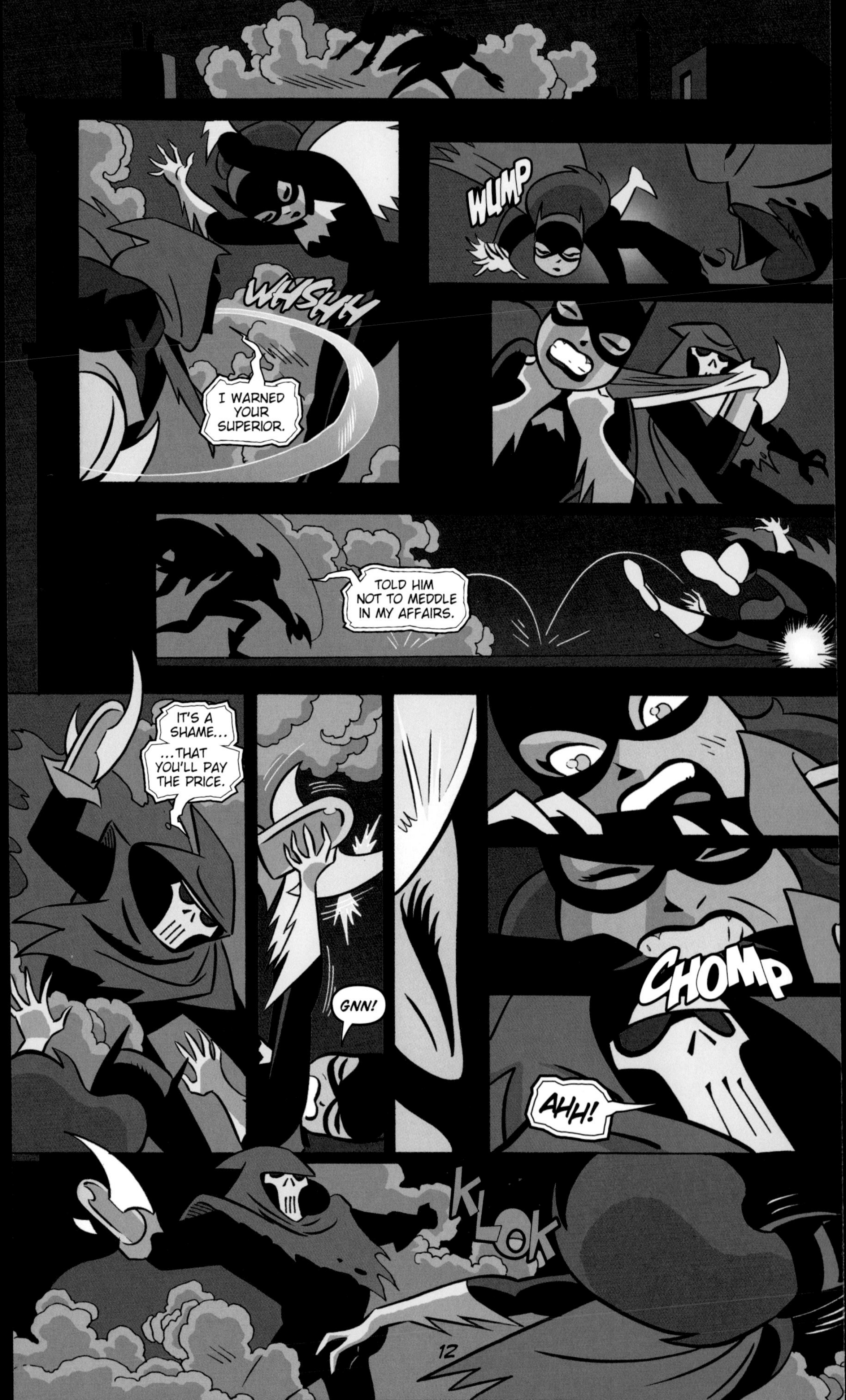

WUMP
WHSHH
I WARNED YOUR SUPERIOR.
TOLD HIM NOT TO MEDDLE IN MY AFFAIRS.
IT'S A SHAME...
...THAT YOU'LL PAY THE PRICE.
GNN!
CHOMP
AHH!
KLOK

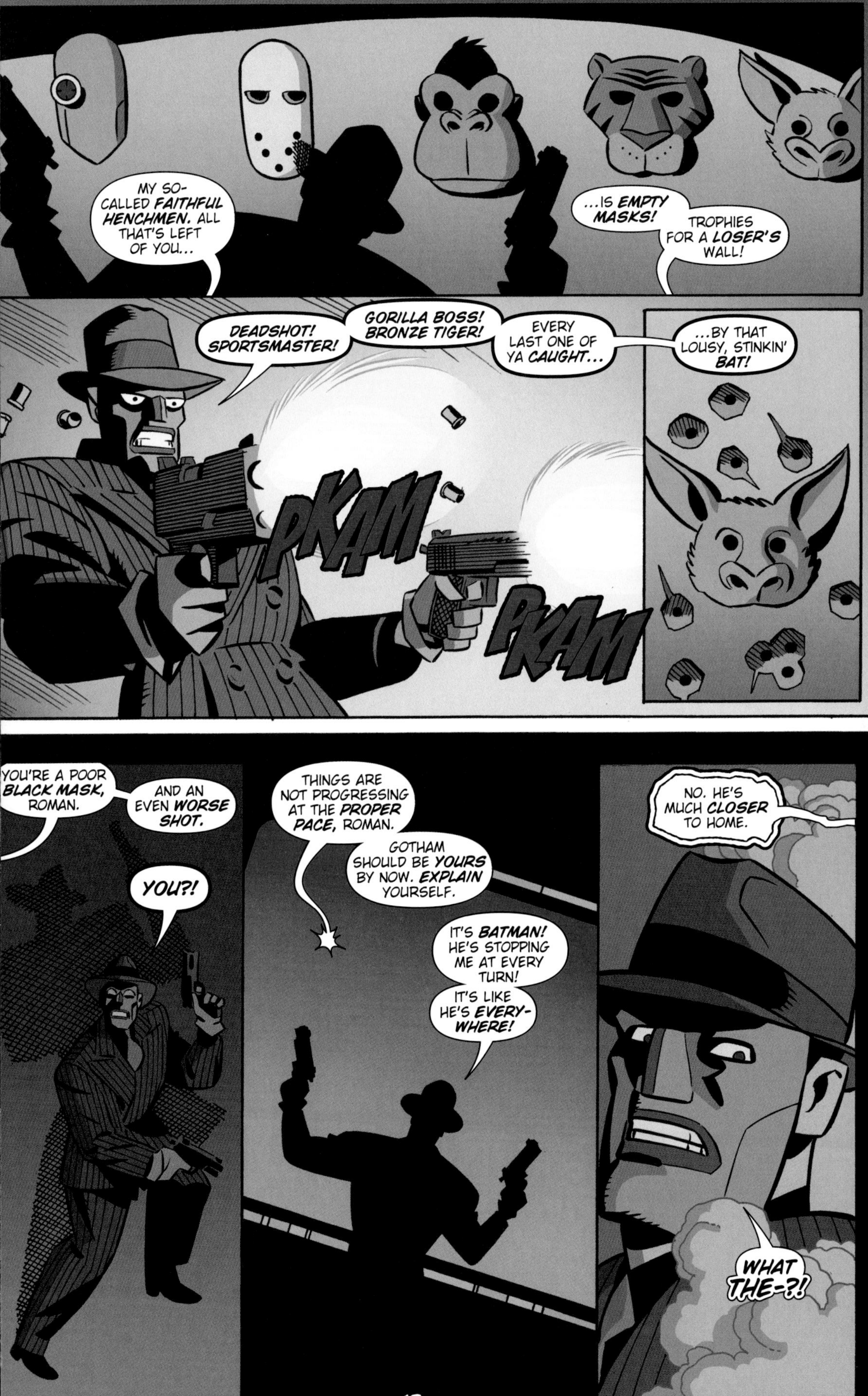

MY SO-CALLED FAITHFUL HENCHMEN. ALL THAT'S LEFT OF YOU...
...IS EMPTY MASKS!
TROPHIES FOR A LOSER'S WALL!
DEADSHOT! SPORTSMASTER!
GORILLA BOSS! BRONZE TIGER!
EVERY LAST ONE OF YA CAUGHT...
...BY THAT LOUSY, STINKIN' BAT!
PKAM
PKAM
YOU'RE A POOR BLACK MASK, ROMAN.
AND AN EVEN WORSE SHOT.
YOU?!
THINGS ARE NOT PROGRESSING AT THE PROPER PACE, ROMAN.
GOTHAM SHOULD BE YOURS BY NOW. EXPLAIN YOURSELF.
IT'S BATMAN! HE'S STOPPING ME AT EVERY TURN!
IT'S LIKE HE'S EVERYWHERE!
NO. HE'S MUCH CLOSER TO HOME.
WHAT THE-?!

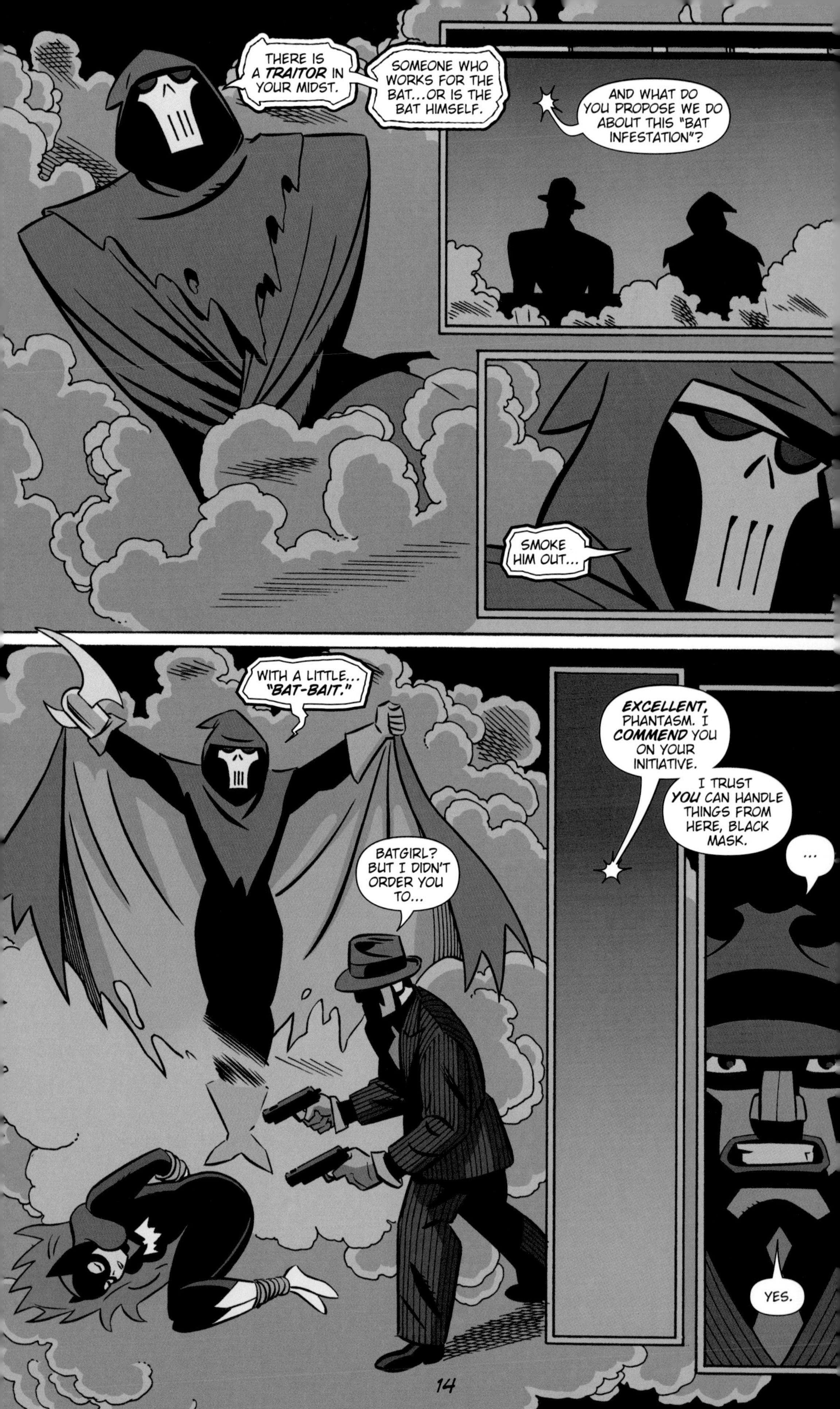
THERE IS A *TRAITOR* IN YOUR MIDST.
SOMEONE WHO WORKS FOR THE BAT...OR IS THE BAT HIMSELF.
AND WHAT DO YOU PROPOSE WE DO ABOUT THIS "BAT INFESTATION"?
SMOKE HIM OUT...
WITH A LITTLE... *"BAT-BAIT."*
BATGIRL? BUT I DIDN'T ORDER YOU TO...
EXCELLENT, PHANTASM. I *COMMEND* YOU ON YOUR INITIATIVE.
I TRUST *YOU* CAN HANDLE THINGS FROM HERE, BLACK MASK.
...
YES.

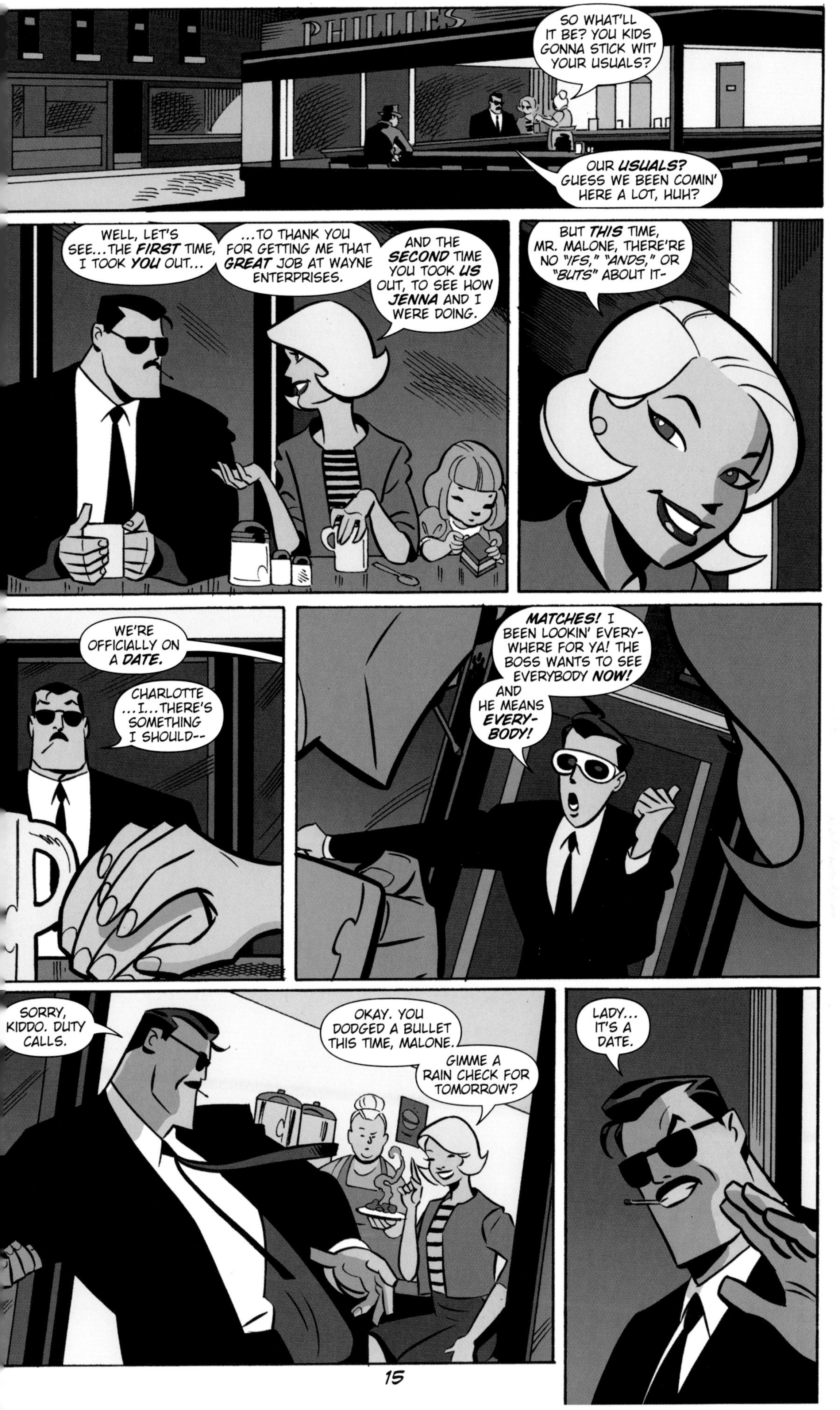

PHILLIES
SO WHAT'LL IT BE? YOU KIDS GONNA STICK WIT' YOUR USUALS?
OUR **USUALS?** GUESS WE BEEN COMIN' HERE A LOT, HUH?
WELL, LET'S SEE... THE **FIRST** TIME, I TOOK **YOU** OUT...
...TO THANK YOU FOR GETTING ME THAT **GREAT** JOB AT WAYNE ENTERPRISES.
AND THE **SECOND** TIME YOU TOOK **US** OUT, TO SEE HOW **JENNA** AND I WERE DOING.
BUT **THIS** TIME, MR. MALONE, THERE'RE NO "*IFS*," "*ANDS*," OR "*BUTS*" ABOUT IT-
WE'RE OFFICIALLY ON A **DATE.**
CHARLOTTE ...I...THERE'S SOMETHING I SHOULD--
MATCHES! I BEEN LOOKIN' EVERYWHERE FOR YA! THE BOSS WANTS TO SEE EVERYBODY **NOW!**
AND HE MEANS **EVERYBODY!**
SORRY, KIDDO. DUTY CALLS.
OKAY. YOU DODGED A BULLET THIS TIME, MALONE.
GIMME A RAIN CHECK FOR TOMORROW?
LADY... IT'S A DATE.

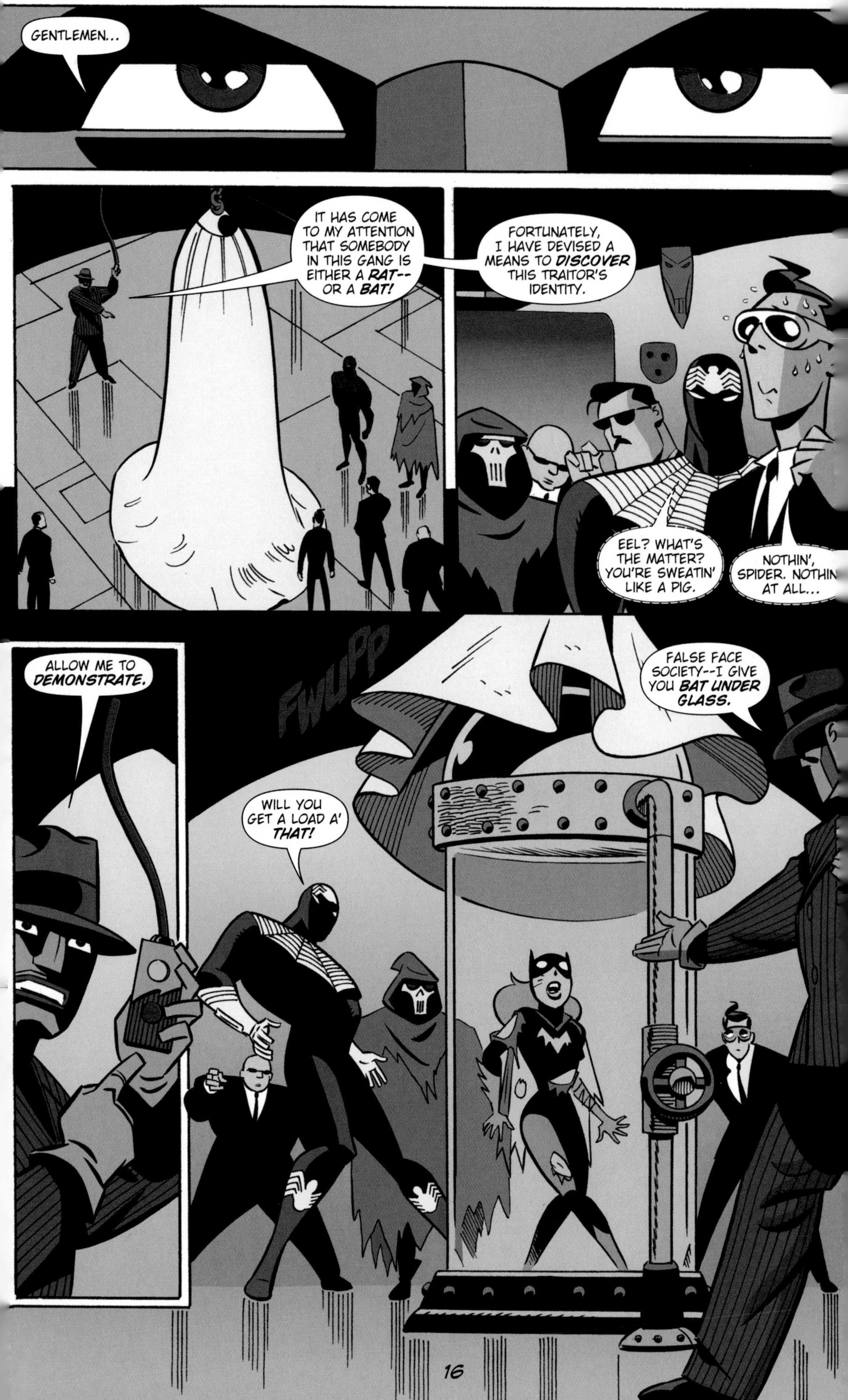

GENTLEMEN...
IT HAS COME TO MY ATTENTION THAT SOMEBODY IN THIS GANG IS EITHER A **RAT--** OR A **BAT!**
FORTUNATELY, I HAVE DEVISED A MEANS TO **DISCOVER** THIS TRAITOR'S IDENTITY.
EEL? WHAT'S THE MATTER? YOU'RE SWEATIN' LIKE A PIG.
NOTHIN', SPIDER. NOTHIN AT ALL...
ALLOW ME TO **DEMONSTRATE.**
FWUPP
FALSE FACE SOCIETY--I GIVE YOU **BAT UNDER GLASS.**
WILL YOU GET A LOAD A' **THAT!**

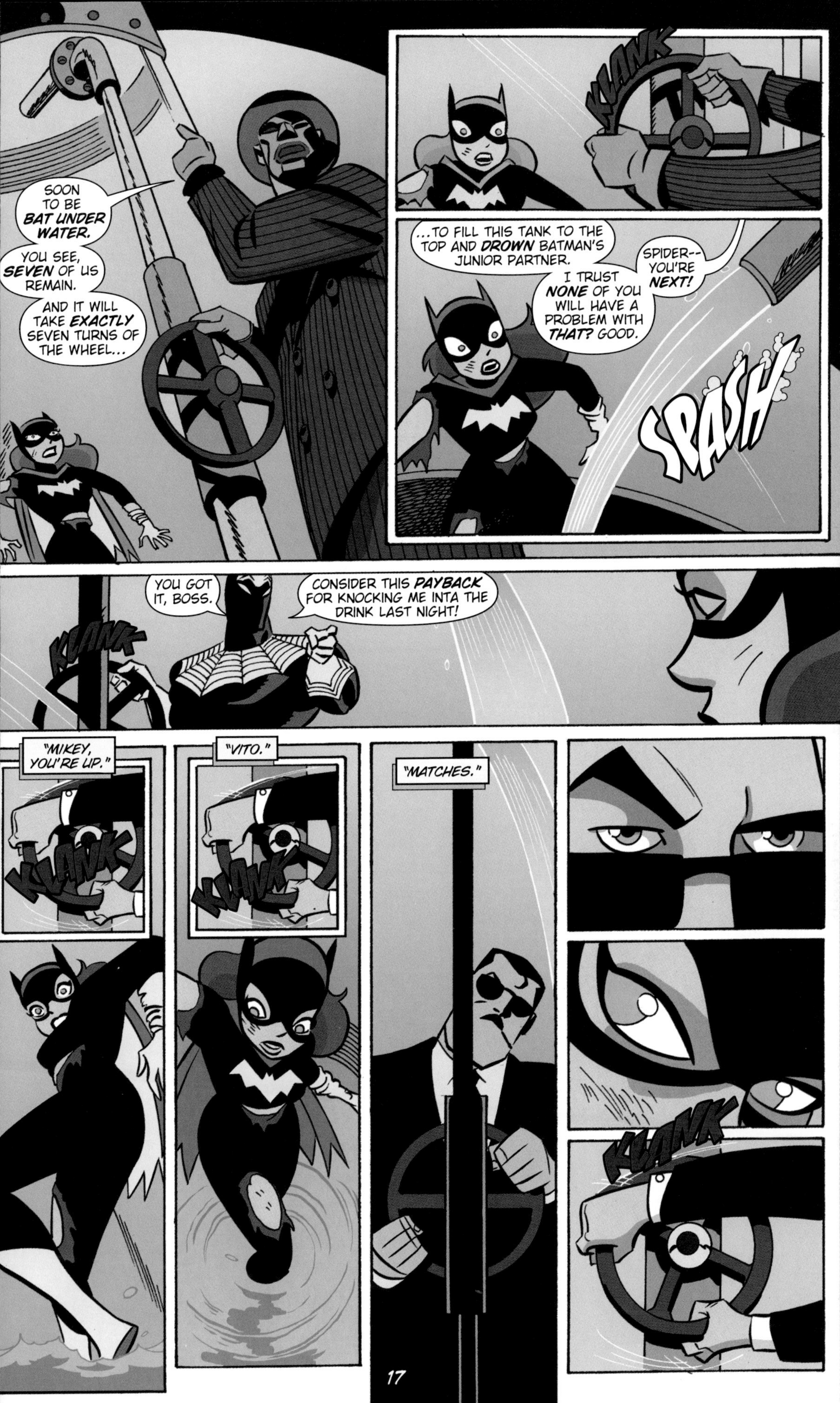

SOON TO BE BAT UNDER WATER.
YOU SEE, SEVEN OF US REMAIN.
AND IT WILL TAKE EXACTLY SEVEN TURNS OF THE WHEEL...
KLANK
...TO FILL THIS TANK TO THE TOP AND DROWN BATMAN'S JUNIOR PARTNER.
I TRUST NONE OF YOU WILL HAVE A PROBLEM WITH THAT? GOOD.
SPIDER-- YOU'RE NEXT!
SPASH
YOU GOT IT, BOSS.
CONSIDER THIS PAYBACK FOR KNOCKING ME INTA THE DRINK LAST NIGHT!
KLANK
"MIKEY, YOU'RE UP."
KLANK
"VITO."
KLANK
"MATCHES."
KLANK

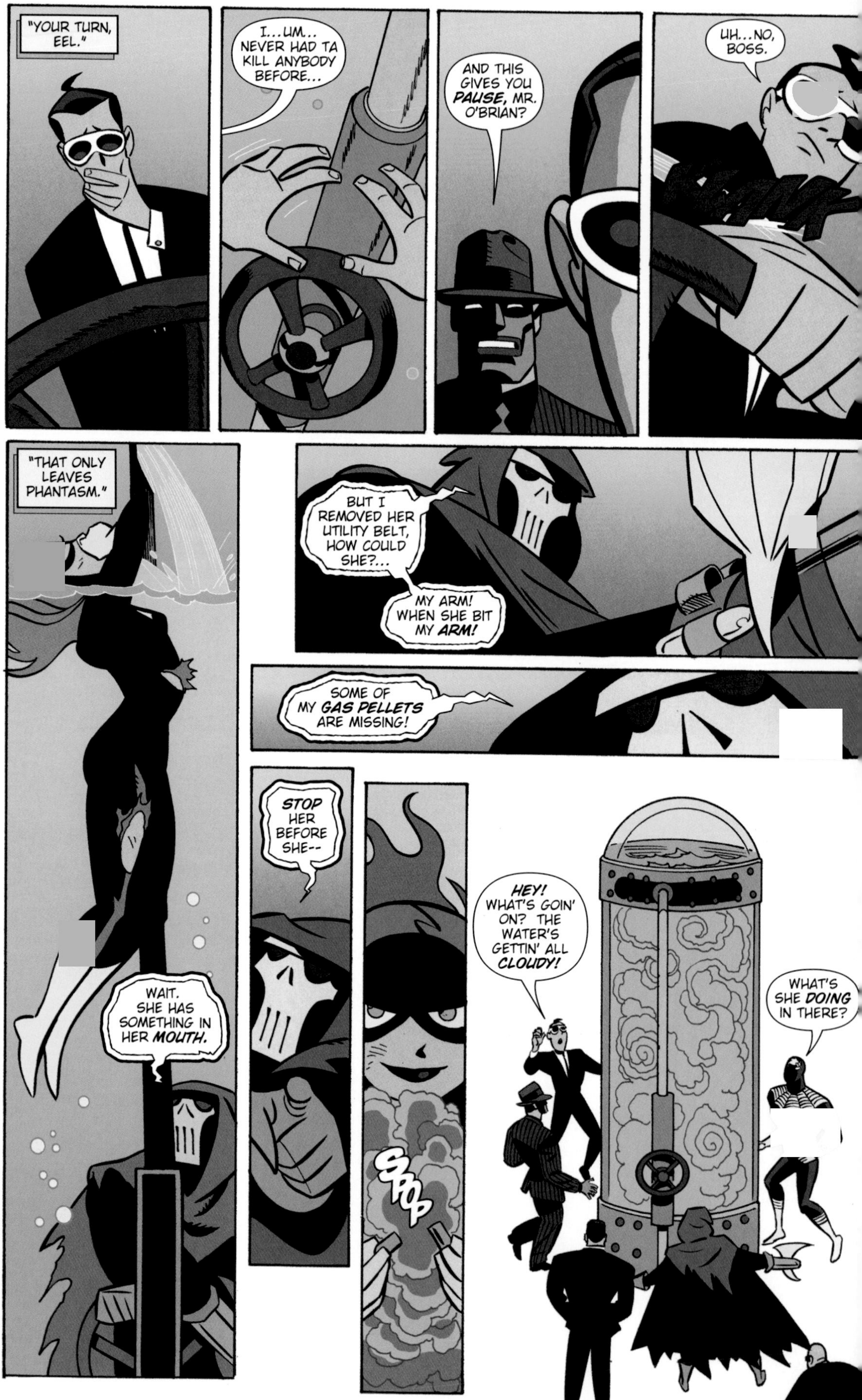
"YOUR TURN, EEL."
I...UM... NEVER HAD TA KILL ANYBODY BEFORE...
AND THIS GIVES YOU PAUSE, MR. O'BRIAN?
UH...NO, BOSS.
"THAT ONLY LEAVES PHANTASM."
BUT I REMOVED HER UTILITY BELT, HOW COULD SHE?...
MY ARM! WHEN SHE BIT MY ARM!
SOME OF MY GAS PELLETS ARE MISSING!
WAIT. SHE HAS SOMETHING IN HER MOUTH.
STOP HER BEFORE SHE--
SPOP
HEY! WHAT'S GOIN' ON? THE WATER'S GETTIN' ALL CLOUDY!
WHAT'S SHE DOING IN THERE?

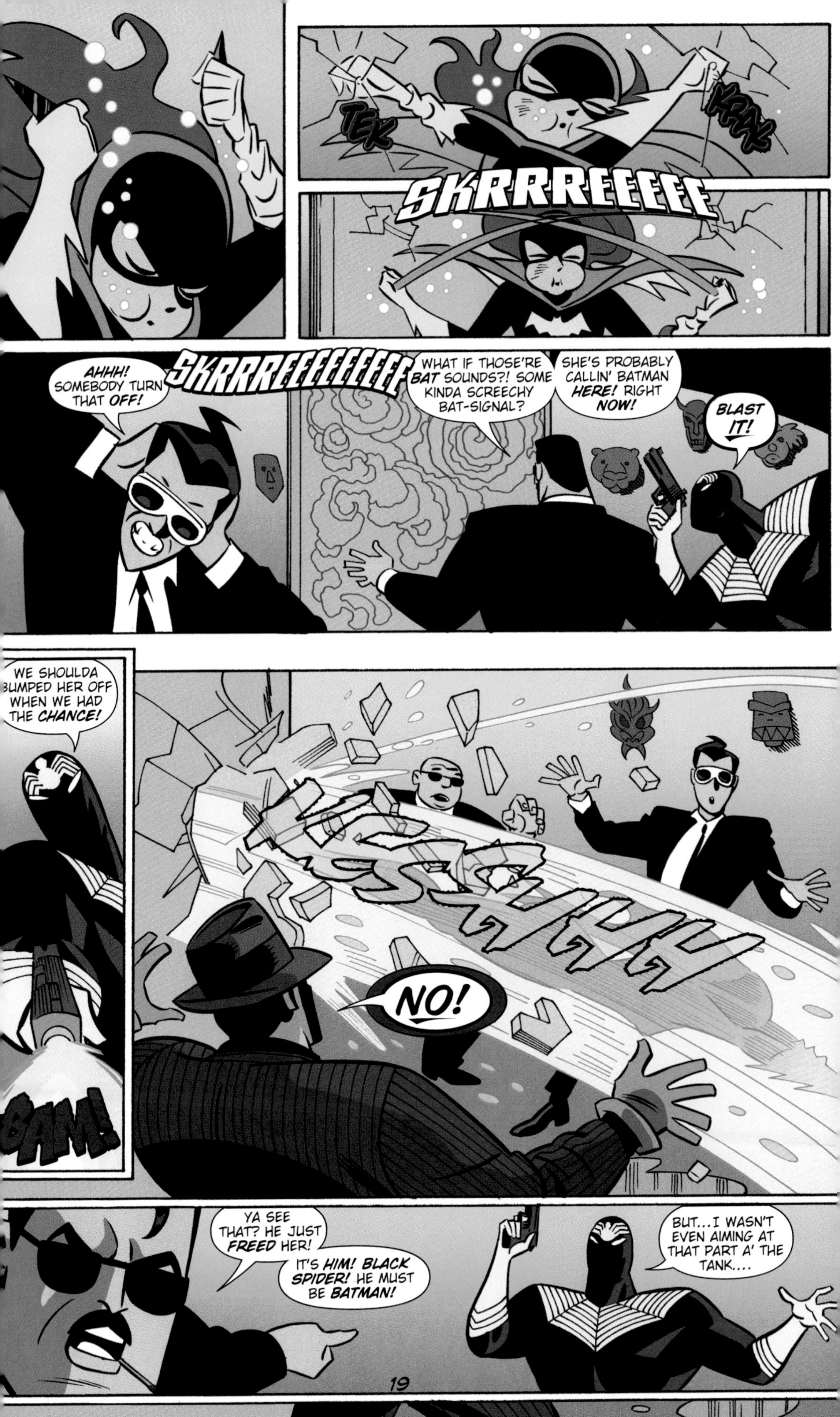
TEK
KRAK
SKRRRREEEEEE
AHHH! SOMEBODY TURN THAT OFF!
SKRRRREEEEEEEEEE
WHAT IF THOSE'RE BAT SOUNDS?! SOME KINDA SCREECHY BAT-SIGNAL?
SHE'S PROBABLY CALLIN' BATMAN HERE! RIGHT NOW!
BLAST IT!
WE SHOULDA BUMPED HER OFF WHEN WE HAD THE CHANCE!
BAM!
NO!
YA SEE THAT? HE JUST FREED HER!
IT'S HIM! BLACK SPIDER! HE MUST BE BATMAN!
BUT... I WASN'T EVEN AIMING AT THAT PART A' THE TANK....

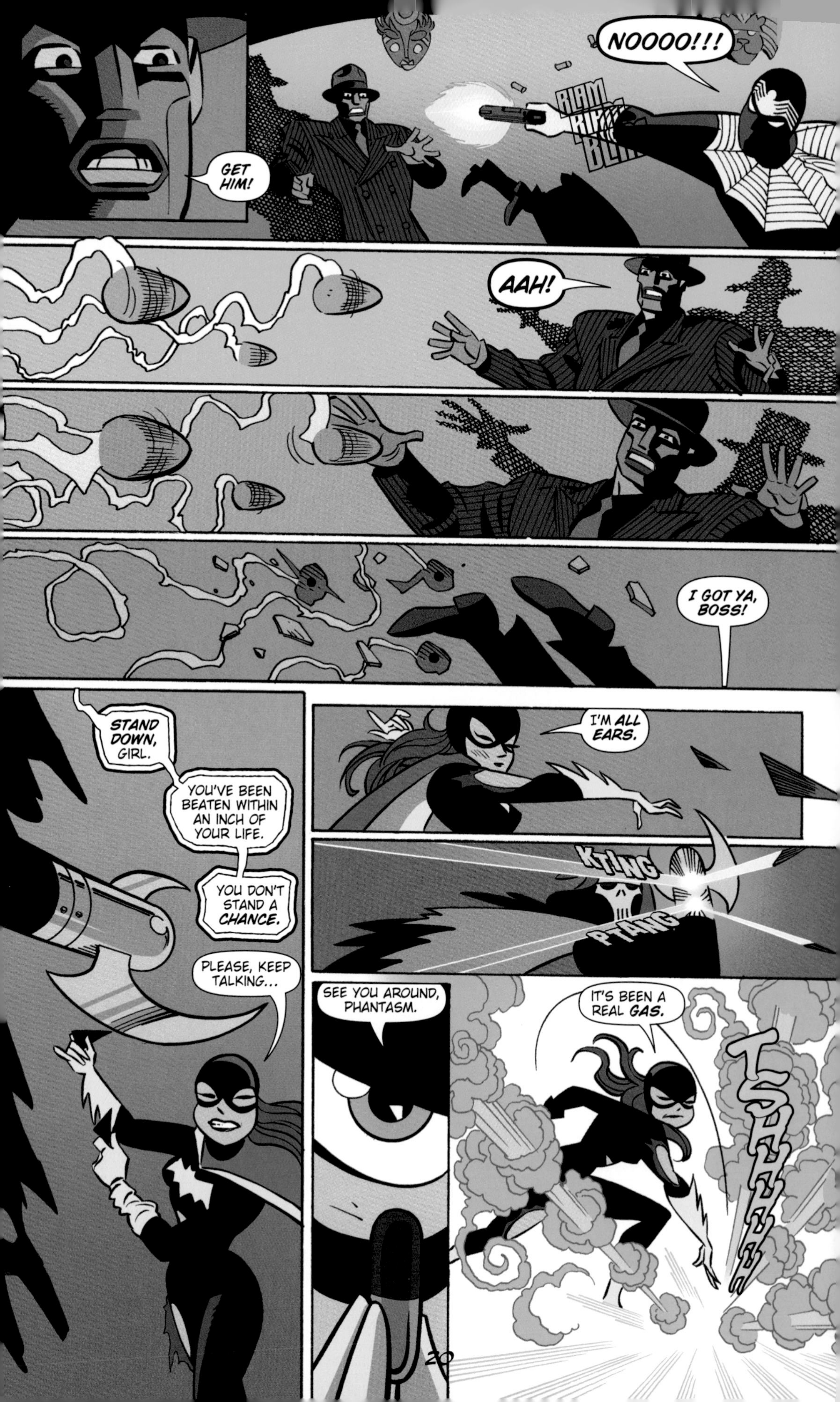
GET HIM!
NOOOO!!!
BLAM
AAH!
I GOT YA, BOSS!
STAND DOWN, GIRL.
YOU'VE BEEN BEATEN WITHIN AN INCH OF YOUR LIFE.
YOU DON'T STAND A CHANCE.
PLEASE, KEEP TALKING...
I'M ALL EARS.
KTING
PTANG
SEE YOU AROUND, PHANTASM.
IT'S BEEN A REAL GAS.

SHE HAD **ANOTHER PELLET!**

AND NOW SHE'S GONE...

HMM. SO **THAT'S** HOW THAT FEELS.

HE MISSED ME! AND **YOU--**

YOU PUSHED ME OUT OF THE WAY, MATCHES... TOOK A **BULLET** FOR ME!

JUST A **SCRATCH,** BOSS.

YOU JUST PROVED YOU'RE THE ONE GUY AROUND HERE I CAN **TRUST.**

TAKE MY HAND, MALONE.

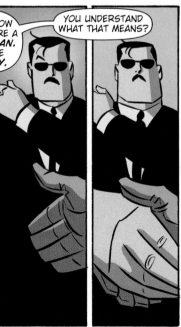

FROM NOW ON, YOU'RE A **MADE MAN.** YOU'RE **FAMILY.**

YOU UNDERSTAND WHAT THAT MEANS?

YES. I KNOW WHAT IT MEANS TO BE PART OF A FAMILY.

END

21

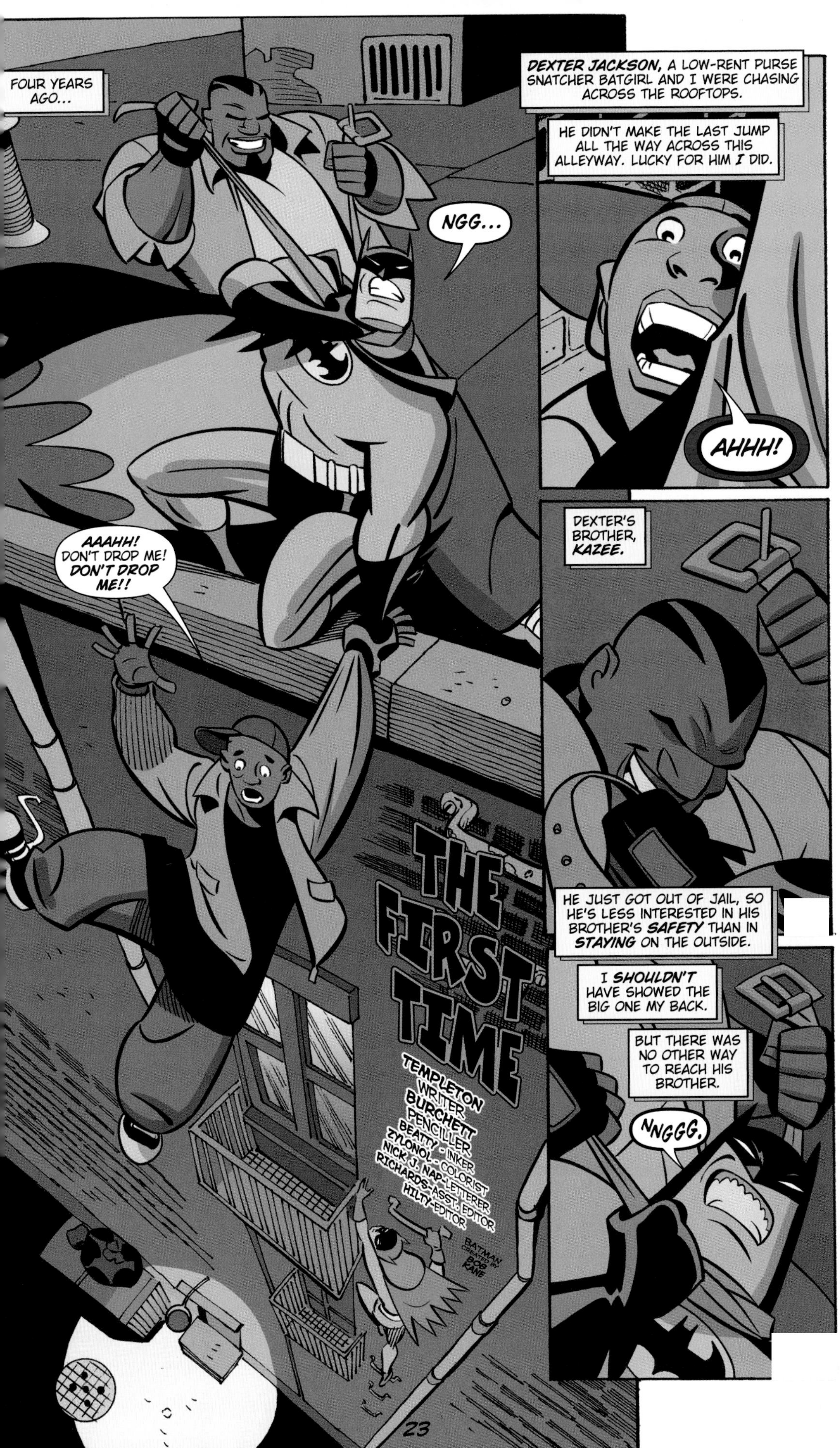
FOUR YEARS AGO...
NGG...
AAAHH! DON'T DROP ME! DON'T DROP ME!!
DEXTER JACKSON, A LOW-RENT PURSE SNATCHER BATGIRL AND I WERE CHASING ACROSS THE ROOFTOPS.
HE DIDN'T MAKE THE LAST JUMP ALL THE WAY ACROSS THIS ALLEYWAY. LUCKY FOR HIM I DID.
AHHH!
DEXTER'S BROTHER, KAZEE.
HE JUST GOT OUT OF JAIL, SO HE'S LESS INTERESTED IN HIS BROTHER'S SAFETY THAN IN STAYING ON THE OUTSIDE.
I SHOULDN'T HAVE SHOWED THE BIG ONE MY BACK.
BUT THERE WAS NO OTHER WAY TO REACH HIS BROTHER.
NNGGG.
THE FIRST TIME
TEMPLETON WRITER
BURCHETT PENCILLER
BEATTY - INKER
ZYLONOL - COLORIST
NICK J. NAP-LETTERER
RICHARDS-ASST. EDITOR
HILTY-EDITOR
BATMAN CREATED BY BOB KANE

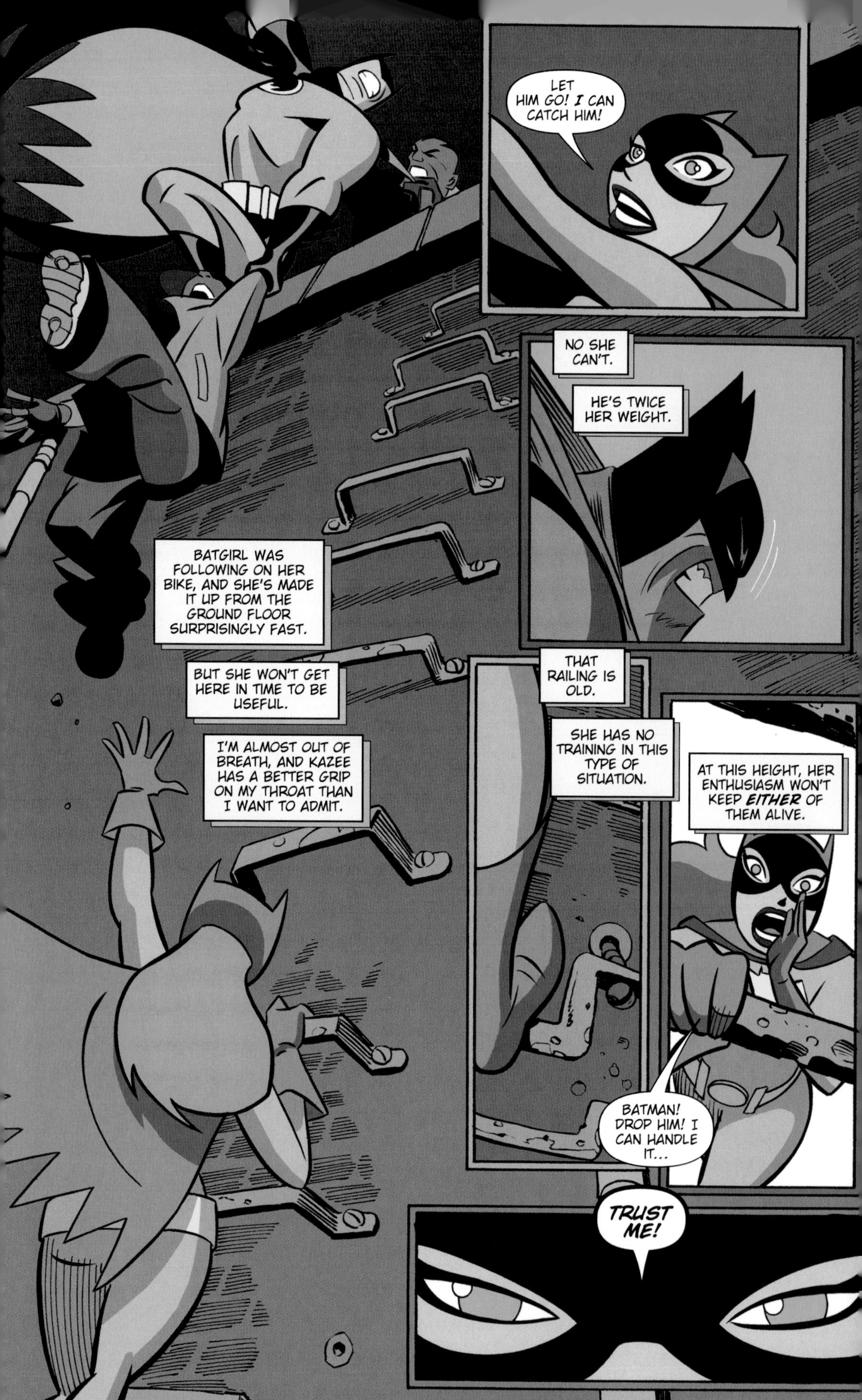
LET HIM GO! I CAN CATCH HIM!
NO SHE CAN'T.
HE'S TWICE HER WEIGHT.
BATGIRL WAS FOLLOWING ON HER BIKE, AND SHE'S MADE IT UP FROM THE GROUND FLOOR SURPRISINGLY FAST.
BUT SHE WON'T GET HERE IN TIME TO BE USEFUL.
I'M ALMOST OUT OF BREATH, AND KAZEE HAS A BETTER GRIP ON MY THROAT THAN I WANT TO ADMIT.
THAT RAILING IS OLD.
SHE HAS NO TRAINING IN THIS TYPE OF SITUATION.
AT THIS HEIGHT, HER ENTHUSIASM WON'T KEEP EITHER OF THEM ALIVE.
BATMAN! DROP HIM! I CAN HANDLE IT...
TRUST ME!

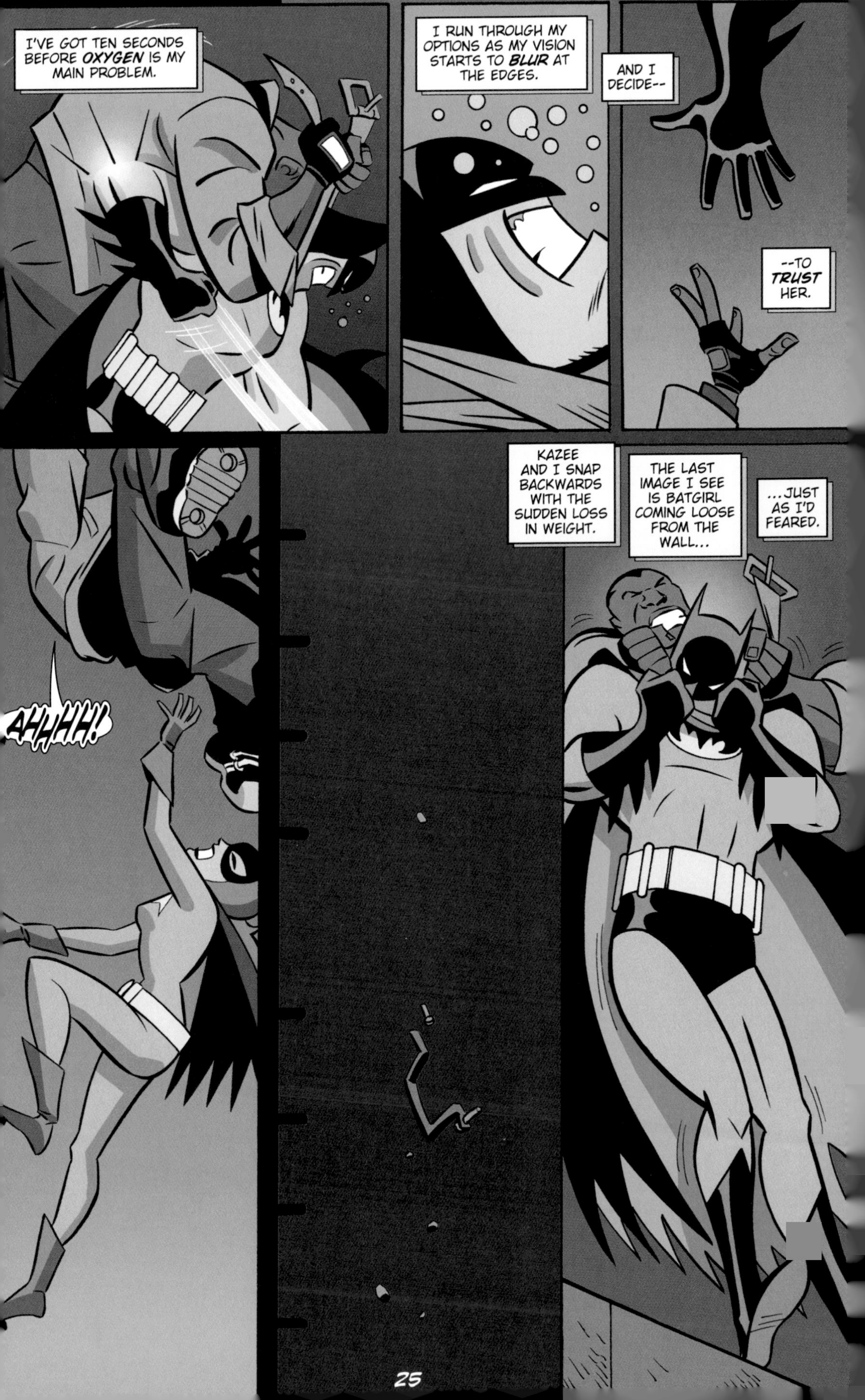
I'VE GOT TEN SECONDS BEFORE OXYGEN IS MY MAIN PROBLEM.
I RUN THROUGH MY OPTIONS AS MY VISION STARTS TO BLUR AT THE EDGES.
AND I DECIDE--
--TO TRUST HER.
AHHHH!
KAZEE AND I SNAP BACKWARDS WITH THE SUDDEN LOSS IN WEIGHT.
THE LAST IMAGE I SEE IS BATGIRL COMING LOOSE FROM THE WALL...
...JUST AS I'D FEARED.

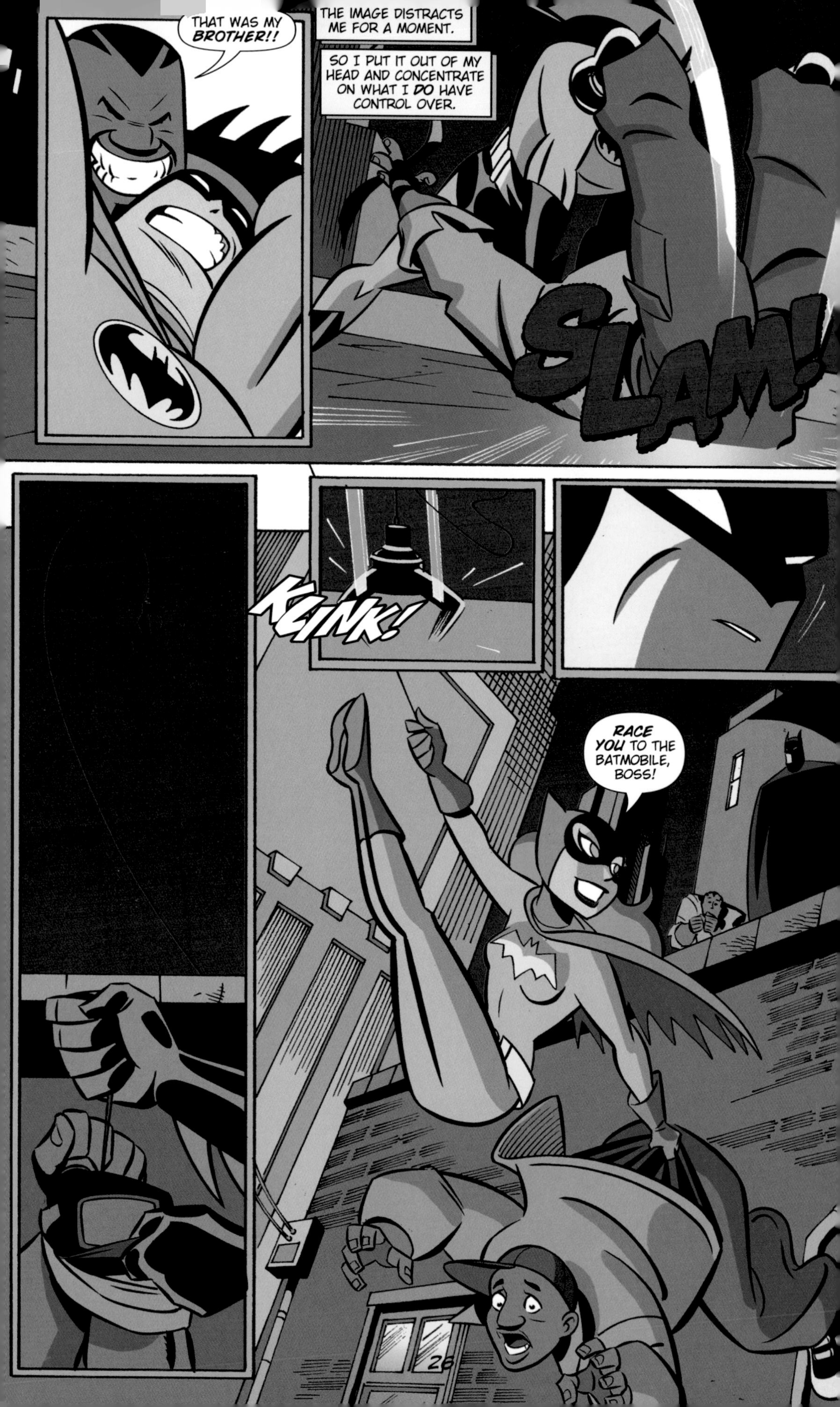
THAT WAS MY BROTHER!!
THE IMAGE DISTRACTS ME FOR A MOMENT.
SO I PUT IT OUT OF MY HEAD AND CONCENTRATE ON WHAT I DO HAVE CONTROL OVER.
SLAM!!
KLINK!
RACE YOU TO THE BATMOBILE, BOSS!

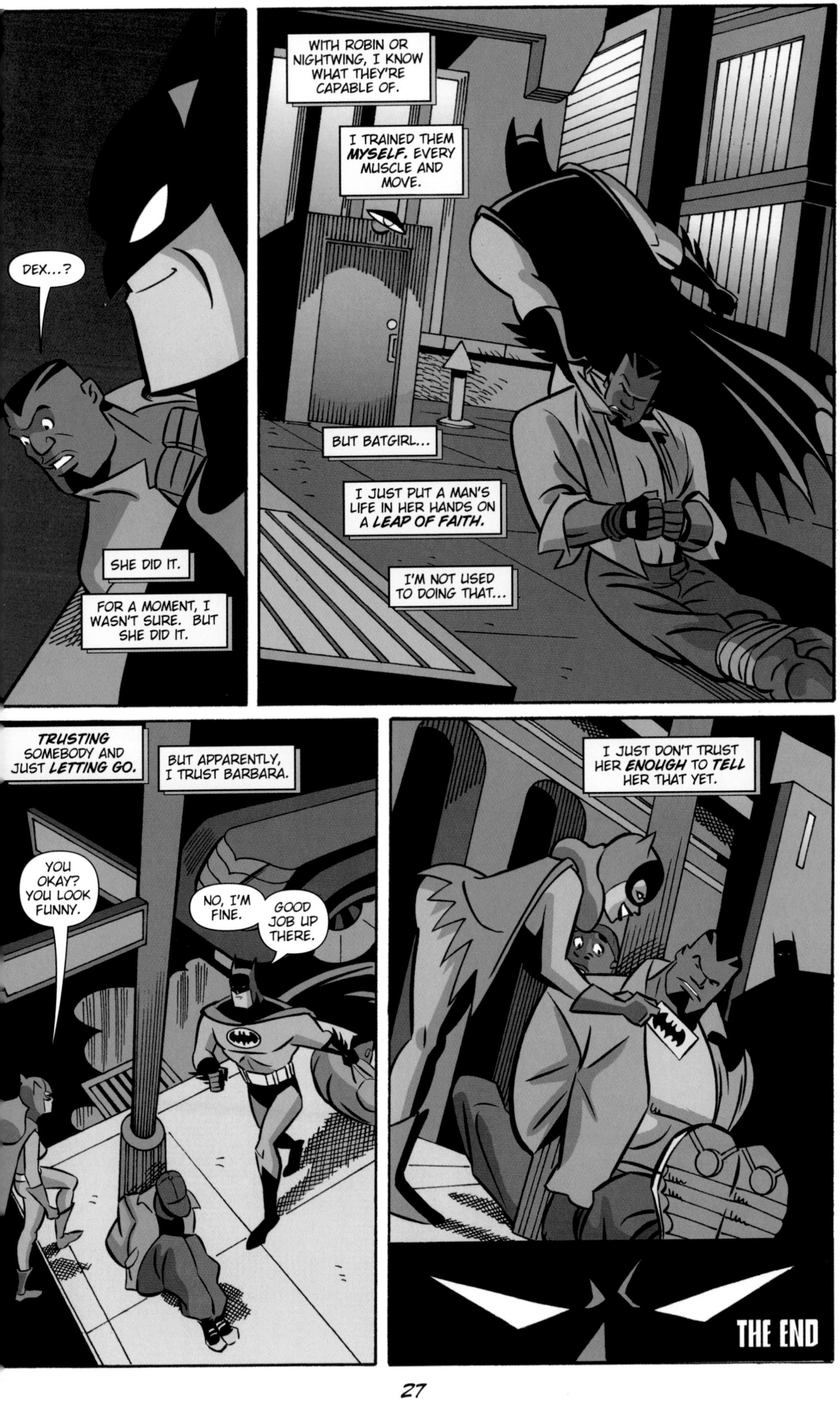

DEX...?
SHE DID IT.
FOR A MOMENT, I WASN'T SURE. BUT SHE DID IT.
WITH ROBIN OR NIGHTWING, I KNOW WHAT THEY'RE CAPABLE OF.
I TRAINED THEM MYSELF. EVERY MUSCLE AND MOVE.
BUT BATGIRL...
I JUST PUT A MAN'S LIFE IN HER HANDS ON A LEAP OF FAITH.
I'M NOT USED TO DOING THAT...
TRUSTING SOMEBODY AND JUST LETTING GO.
BUT APPARENTLY, I TRUST BARBARA.
YOU OKAY? YOU LOOK FUNNY.
NO, I'M FINE.
GOOD JOB UP THERE.
I JUST DON'T TRUST HER ENOUGH TO TELL HER THAT YET.
THE END

CREATORS

DAN SLOTT WRITER

Dan Slott is a comics writer best known for his work on DC Comics' Arkham Asylum, and, for Marvel, The Avengers and the Amazing Spider-Man.

RICK BURCHETT PENCILLER

Rick Burchett has worked as a comics artist for more than 25 years. He has received the comics industry's Eisner Award three times, Spain's Haxtur Award, and he has been nominated for the Eagle Award. Rick lives with his wife and two sons in Missouri, USA.

TERRY BEATTY INKER

For more than ten years, Terry Beatty was the main inker of DC Comics' "animated-style" Batman comics, including The Batman Strikes. More recently, he worked on *Return to Perdition*, a graphic novel for DC's Vertigo Crime.

LEE LOUGHRIDGE COLORIST

Lee Loughridge has been working in comics for more than fifteen years. He currently lives in sunny California in a tent on the beach.

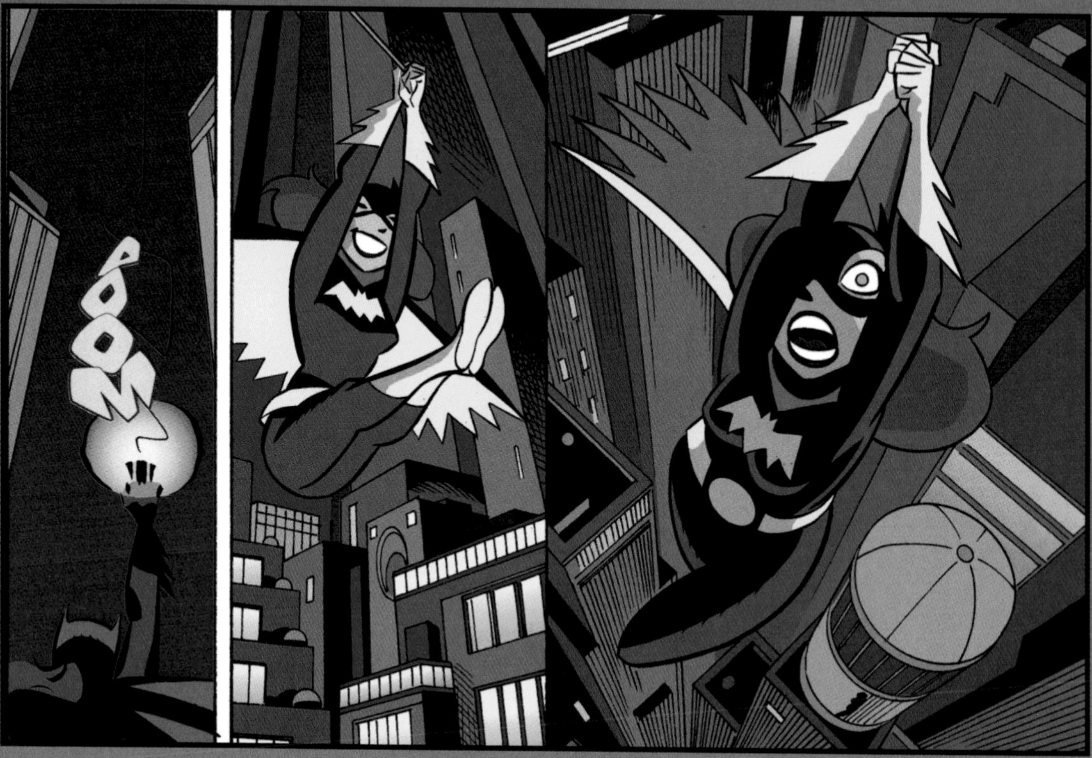
POOM

GLOSSARY

bisque (BISSK)--a thick cream soup, especially of puréed shellfish or vegetables.

commend (kuh-MEND)--praise

deliberately (duh-LIB-er-uht-lee)--intentionally or on purpose

devised (di-VIZED)--thought something up or invented something

honor (ON-ur)--to give praise or an award, or to keep an agreement

infestation (in-feh-STAY-shuhn)--a harassing or troublesome invasion

initiative (i-NISH-ee-uh-tiv)--if you take initiative, you do what is necessary without other people telling you to do it

leap of faith (LEEP OF FAYTH)--believing in or doing something despite a lack of evidence or proof

shame (SHAME)--dishonor or disgrace

smuggling (SMUHG-uhl-ing)--taking something out of its place in secret

superior (suh-PEER-ee-ur)--above average in quality or ability, or a higher rank or position

sustain (suh-STAYN)--if something sustains you, it gives you the energy and strength needed to keep going

BATMAN GLOSSARY

Batgirl: Barbara Gordon, a.k.a. Batgirl, is one of Batman's most trusted crimefighting partners.

Batboat: a submersible vehicle capable of high speed water travel.

Black Spider: a capable assassin and member of the False Face Society.

Black Mask: also known as Roman Sionis, Black Mask is a ruthless businessman and criminal boss of the Gotham underworld.

False Face Society: an organization of masked criminals who work for Black Mask. Each member of the Society chooses a mask to wear to disguise their true identity.

Matches Malone: a two-bit gangster Batman poses as to infiltrate criminal organizations.

Phantasm: despite posing as a man, Phantasm is actually Andrea Beaumont, a deadly martial artist who wields her scythe with expert skill.

Utility Belt: each member of the Batfamily owns a Utlity Belt that suits their specific crimefighting needs. Each belt contains several compartments with many gadgets that are useful in fighting crime.

VISUAL QUESTIONS & PROMPTS

1. Why are these particular masks hanging on Black Mask's wall?

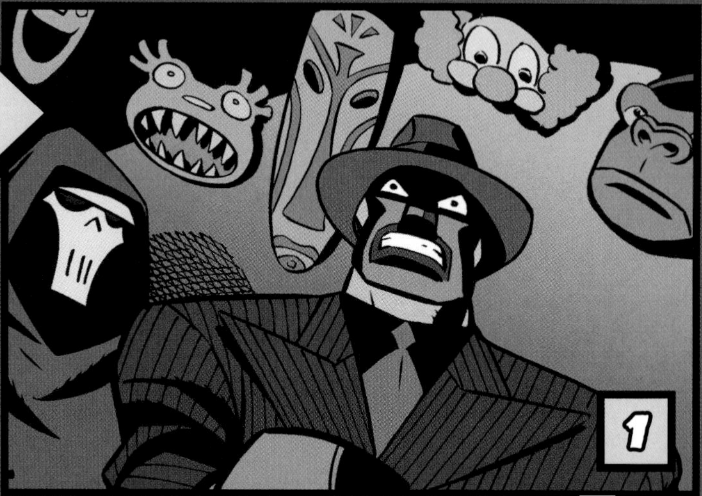
1

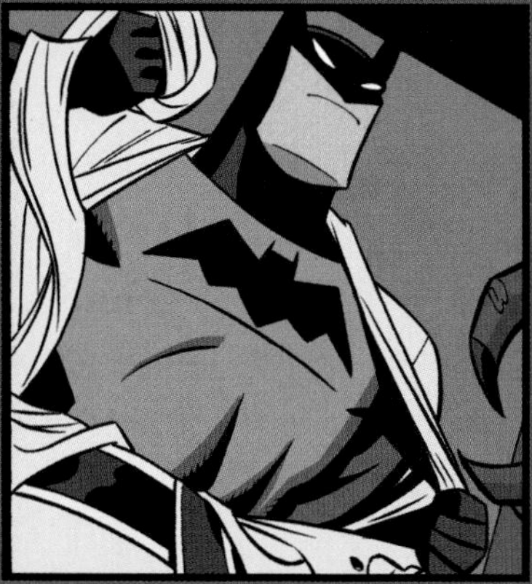

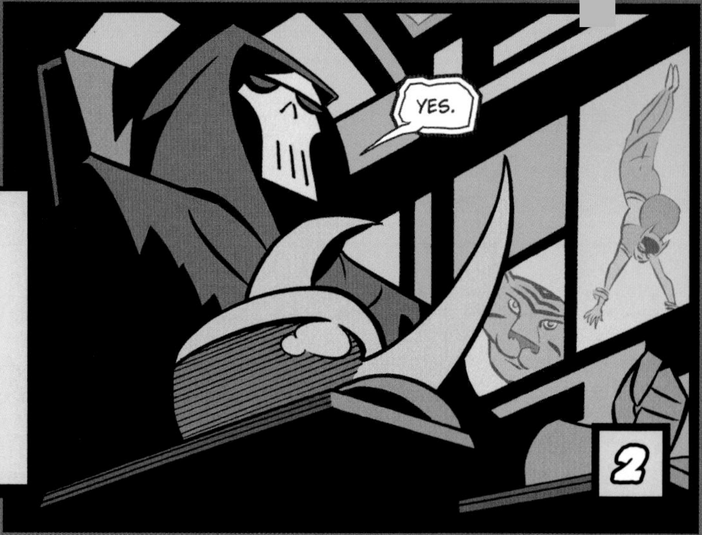
YES.
2

2. Phantasm's speech balloons look strange. Why is that? Read the character's bio on the previous spread for clues.

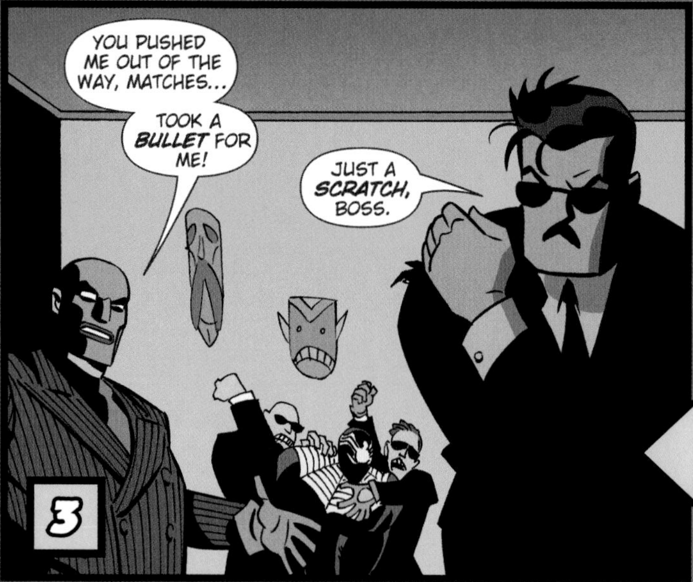
YOU PUSHED ME OUT OF THE WAY, MATCHES...
TOOK A *BULLET* FOR ME!
JUST A *SCRATCH*, BOSS.
3

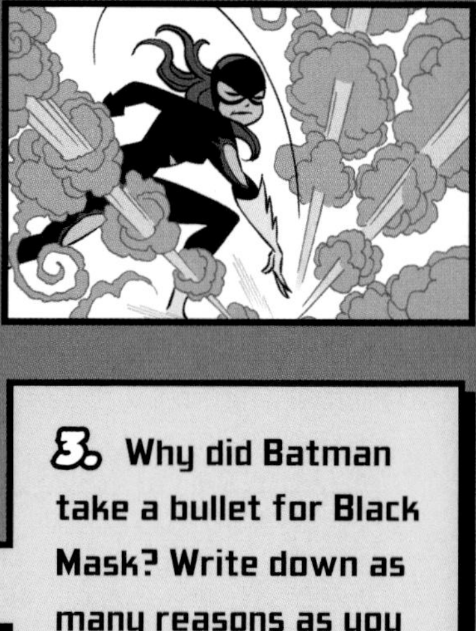

3. Why did Batman take a bullet for Black Mask? Write down as many reasons as you can come up with.

4. Batman is a master of going undercover. Find three specific panels times in this book where Batman manages to trick criminals into thinking he's someone else.

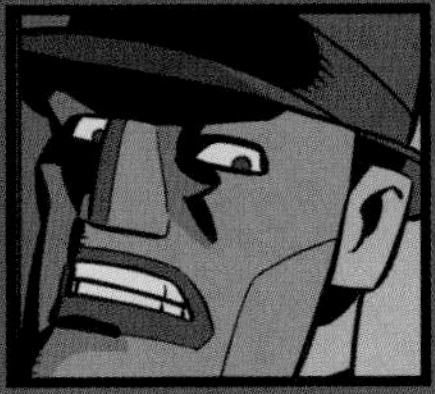

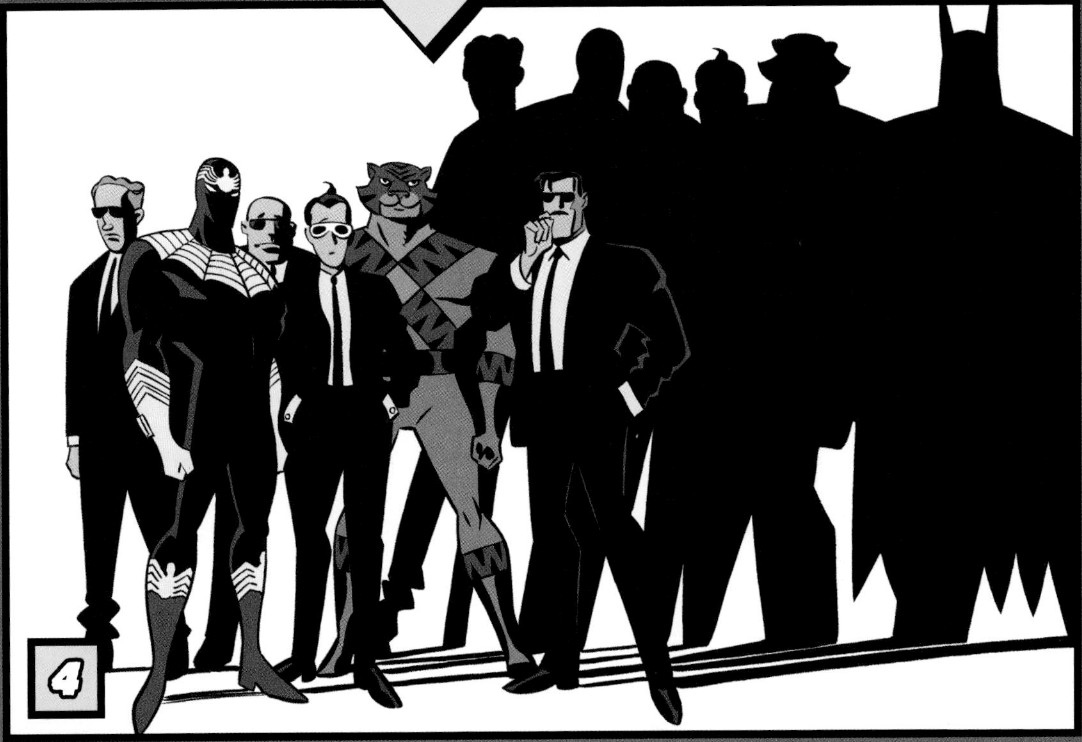
4

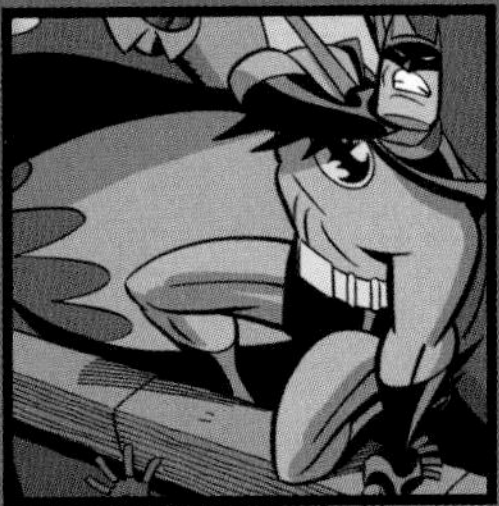

5. Describe in your own words the path of movement Batgirl takes in this panel, starting with her fall and ending with her landing.

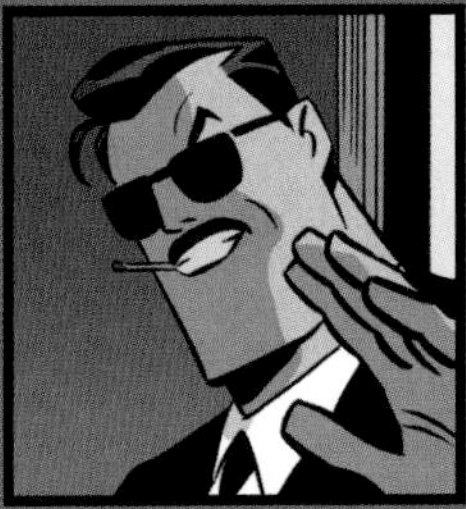

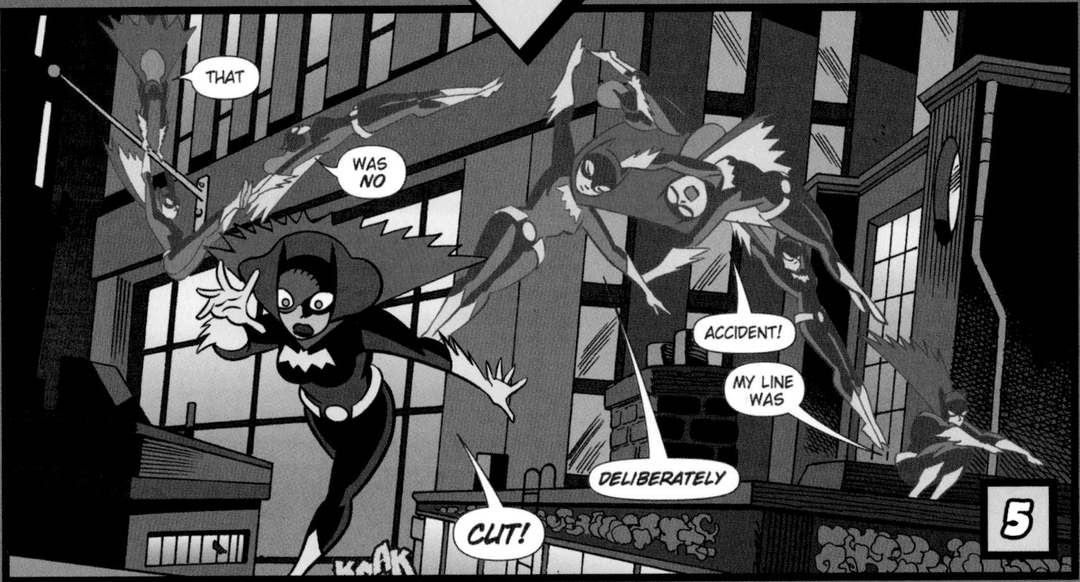
THAT
WAS NO
ACCIDENT!
MY LINE WAS
DELIBERATELY
CUT!
5

BATMAN ADVENTURES